Of course, there was the little matter of Kurt Callahan.

But once the grand opening of his new store was past he'd be going home, and that interference would be gone as well. And with him out of the way her peace of mind would be restored and she could get down to work...for a while, at least.

The nerve of the man, threatening to tell her new boss what had happened between them all those years ago. Of course he wouldn't actually do it, because he'd be the one who ended up looking bad. Still...Lissa had thought she was long over the sting of the single evening she'd spent with him. Even in the cloakroom last night she hadn't entirely lost her perspective. But that was before she'd had to deal with him on such a personal level, and now all the feelings had come flashing back: the frustration and the anger, the hurt, the desolation and—yes, the attraction too...

Leigh Michaels has always been a writer, composing dreadful poetry when she was just four years old and dictating it to her long-suffering older sister. She started writing romance in her teens, and burned six full manuscripts before submitting her work to a publisher. Now, with more than 70 novels to her credit, she also teaches romance writing seminars at universities, writers' conferences, and on the Internet. Leigh loves to hear from readers. You may contact her at PO Box 935, Ottumwa, Iowa 52501, USA, or visit her website: leigh@leighmichaels.com

Recent titles by the same author:

ASSIGNMENT: TWINS
PART-TIME FIANCÉ
THE TAKEOVER BID

THE TYCOON'S PROPOSAL

BY
LEIGH MICHAELS

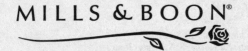

MILLS & BOON®

For Alexandra, who knows why

First published in Great Britain 2006
Harlequin Mills & Boon Limited,
Eton House, 18-24 Paradise Road, Richmond, Surrey TW9 1SR

© Leigh Michaels 2006

ISBN-13: 978 0 263 84911 0
ISBN-10:   0 263 84911 2

Set in Times Roman 12 on 14 pt.
02-0706-56747

Printed and bound in Spain
by Litografia Rosés, S.A., Barcelona

CHAPTER ONE

LONG BEFORE THE banquet was over, Kurt was feeling restless. Why couldn't people just say thank you and leave it at that? If he hadn't wanted to donate all that equipment he wouldn't have done it. So why should he be required to sit at a head table and smile for what seemed hours while everyone from the university's president on down expressed their appreciation?

As if she'd read his mind, his grandmother leaned toward him and whispered, "Most people who donate things enjoy the public recognition. You look as if you have a toothache." She gave an approving nod toward the podium and applauded politely.

Kurt hadn't noticed until then that yet another speaker had finally wound to his interminable conclusion. He rose, made the obligatory half-bow toward the speaker, gave the audience another self-deprecating smile, and hoped to high heaven that they were done.

Apparently they were—or else the audience had finally had enough too, for most of them were on their feet. "At last," he said under his breath.

"It's only been an hour," his grandmother said. "You really must learn some patience."

Now that it was almost finished he could begin to see some humor in the situation. "I didn't hear you saying anything about the need to be patient while I was getting myself established in business, Gran. In fact, I seem to remember you egging me on by saying you wanted me to hurry up and get rich enough to buy you a mink coat."

"What I said," she reminded him crisply, "was that I wanted a mink coat and a great-grandchild before I died, and since I was perfectly able to buy my own mink coat you should concentrate on the great-grandchild."

He suppressed a grin at how easily she'd stepped into the trap. "Well, these people have been telling you all evening how great your grandchild is. So the way I see it, now that you know I'm perfect you have nothing left to complain about."

She smiled. "And here I thought you brought me tonight only because you couldn't decide which of the young women on your list deserved the laurels."

She wasn't far wrong about that, Kurt admitted. He could think of half a dozen women who would have been pleased to attend this event with him—unexciting as it had turned out to be. But that was part of the problem, of course. *Invite a woman to a party and she understands it's just a date. Invite her to a boring banquet in your honor and she starts thinking you must be serious.*

His grandmother was looking beyond him. "Don't look now, but here comes another one."

And if you take your grandmother to the banquet instead, he thought, *the hopefuls start coming out of the walls.*

From the corner of his eye, he spotted a woman coming toward them. This one was blond—but only the hair color seemed to change; they were all young, sleek, improbably curvy, with perfect pert noses. It was as if someone had put a Barbie doll on the copy machine and hit the *enlarge* button.

There had been two of them before they'd even sat down to dinner—fluttering over to enthuse about how wonderful he was to make such a huge contribution, obviously thinking that the way to any man's heart was through his ego. If Kurt had started the evening with any inclination to think himself special—which he hadn't—that would have been enough to cure him.

"Time to get out of here." He offered his arm to his grandmother.

Outside the banquet room, a few people were milling about, buttoning winter coats and wrapping scarves before leaving the warm student union for the wintry outdoors.

"There's a chair," Kurt said. "And isn't that your friend Marian? You can talk to her while I get your coat."

The cloakroom counter was busy, and only one attendant was on duty. When they'd arrived the crowd had been trickling in and there had been two people manning the cloakroom. Now that everyone wanted to leave at once there was just one. Bad planning, Kurt thought.

Several young men were clustered at one end of the counter. Kurt recognized some of them as the athletes who had helped to demonstrate the equipment he had donated for the student union's new gym before all the dignitaries had trooped up to the banquet room to start the congratulations. Kurt looked past them and saw why they were hanging around—the attendant on duty was female, young, and not at all hard on the eyes.

He fidgeted with his claim ticket as he waited his turn, and he watched the young woman. She wasn't conventionally pretty at all. She was far too thin for her height, he thought. Her eyes were much too big for her face, and her auburn hair was cropped shorter than many men's. And the anonymous uniform of a server—black trousers, boxy white tuxedo shirt, bow tie—did little for her slim figure. But she was stunning, nevertheless, the sort of woman who drew gazes, and attention, and interest.

The athletes were certainly interested. Every

time she came back to the counter with a coat, one or more of them had a comment. Some of the remarks she ignored, some she smiled at, some brought a quip in return.

She's leading them on, Kurt thought. Not that he cared whether she flirted with the customers, as long as she continued to work efficiently through the crowd. He eyed the small glass jar which sat discreetly at one end of the counter, hinting that tips would be welcome. It was half full of bills and coins. No doubt the occasional flirtation increased the evening's take.

Before long the foyer was emptying out, but the athletes were still hanging on. "When do you get off duty?" one of them asked the attendant.

"Hard to say," the young woman said. "With all these people to take care of, it might be another hour."

"I'll hang around for a while," the athlete said. "You'll need a ride home because it's snowing."

"No, thanks. I like snow. Besides—" She checked the number on a ticket and went to the farthest rack to get an overcoat.

By the time she came back the athlete had apparently thought it through. "I know. You've got a boyfriend to come and get you."

She flashed a smile. "What do you think?"

"I'll save him the trouble," the athlete offered.

The young woman held out a hand for Kurt's claim check, but she didn't look at him because she was still studying the athlete. "Tell you what," she said. "I'll give you a phone number. Call in an hour—just in case he hasn't shown up."

The athlete was practically salivating. He grabbed for a discarded napkin that lay on the counter and thrust it at her. She scribbled something and pushed it back.

"Is this your cell phone?" the athlete asked. "Where are you from, anyway? This isn't a local number."

She didn't seem to hear. She looked up from the ticket she held and smiled at Kurt. "Be right back."

Now he understood what had drawn the athletes. She might be skinny and big-eyed and boyish, but when she smiled—even that polite, almost meaningless smile of acknowledgment—the room instantly grew ten degrees warmer. Or maybe it wasn't the entire room which heated up but just the men in her general vicinity. That would certainly explain why the athletes' tongues were all hanging out.

There was something almost familiar about that smile....

But then, practically everything Kurt had seen in the last few days had given him a sensation of déjà vu. It was because he was back on campus, that was all. It had been a long time since graduation. And there were a lot of memories—good and bad—to dredge up...

She was gone for quite a while, and he started to wonder if she was ever coming back. Kurt leaned against the counter and crossed his arms, and the young men, after a few wary glances in his direction, moved away.

She returned with his grandmother's mink and his own dark gray cashmere overcoat. "Sorry to take so long. I had the mink tucked away clear in the back, where it would be safer. It's too beautiful to risk." She ran a hand over the fur before she passed it across the counter.

Kurt laid the mink down and put on his own coat. "I seem to have driven away your admirers."

"Oh, that's all right," she said lightly. "If they'd hung around here much longer they'd have gotten me in trouble with the boss."

"I hope I didn't discourage the young man from calling."

"Probably not." She didn't sound excited at the possibility. "I hope he likes listening to the time and temperature recording in Winnipeg."

He wasn't surprised that it hadn't really been her number she'd handed out. But why had she admitted it to him—a complete stranger?

Three guesses, Callahan, he told himself. *Because she's after bigger game, so she's making sure you know the athlete's not important.*

No wonder he'd had that flash of thinking she looked familiar. One predatory feminine gaze was pretty much like another in his experience.

Her fingertips went out to caress the fur, still

draped across the counter. "Careful where you leave that. We get a soft drink spilled every now and then around here, and I'd hate to see that beautiful coat get sticky." She looked up at him through her lashes, with something like speculation in her gaze.

She's debating what kind of approach will be most successful, he thought. Well, maybe he'd make it easy for her.

He picked up the mink, and then turned back as if struck by an afterthought. "I wonder…." He did his best to sound naive. "If *I* asked for your phone number, would you pass me off with time and temperature in Winnipeg?"

She looked at him for a long moment and her eyes seemed to get even bigger.

Calculating my bank balance, no doubt.

"Wouldn't dream of it." She reached for his claim ticket, which was still lying on the counter, flipped it over, pulled a felt-tipped marker from her pocket, and wrote a number on the back side. "Here you go."

It certainly wasn't the time and temperature in Winnipeg, Kurt saw, because she hadn't added an area code. Not that he'd expected anything else. Now she had connected him with the expensive coat, there was no doubt in his mind that she had given him a real number.

Still, he had to admit to a trickle of disappointment, because somehow he'd expected more subtlety from this young woman.

So much for subtlety. He wondered how long she'd wait for him to call. Too bad that he'd never get to find out.

He dropped a substantial tip into the glass jar, and didn't look back as he crossed the lobby to where his grandmother was talking to a white-haired dowager. "I'll meet you here for lunch tomorrow, Marian," his grandmother said. "And perhaps you can bring that young friend of yours to tea sometime in the next few days? Kurt's staying with me through Christmas, you know."

Kurt held his tongue until they were outside, protected from the falling snow by the awning as they waited for the valet to bring his car around. The street was already covered, with soft ruts starting to form in the traffic lanes. Flakes the size of quarters were falling slowly and almost silently. "Marian's young friend is a female, of course," he said.

"Now, what would make you say that, dear?" His grandmother looked meditatively at the street. "Falling snow is almost hypnotic, really. It's such a relief in weather like this to be in the hands of an exceptionally good driver."

"What big fibs you tell, Granny," Kurt said dryly.

His Jaguar pulled up under the awning. As he reached into his pocket for a tip for the valet his fingers brushed the claim ticket. Maybe he should give that to the valet, too, he thought. No—the kid might think he'd been handed a reward, and no inexperienced young guy deserved the kind of trouble that woman represented.

Kurt decided he'd tear the ticket up and throw it away when he got home. Or maybe he'd keep it for a while, just as a reminder of how careful a guy needed to be these days. Not because he'd ever be tempted to use it.

The ticket slid from his fingers and drifted downward like one of the snowflakes. The small card was warm from his pocket, and the first huge flake which collided with it melted instantly and blurred the ink. He dived after it, and his dress shoe slipped on an icy spot, almost careening him head-first into a drift.

Even as he was scrambling to keep his balance in the snow he told himself it was stupid to care whether he could still read a number that he had no intention of calling. But it burned itself into his brain anyway, as he picked up the ticket and carefully blotted the snowflake away. The handwriting was strong, clear, and neat, with each numeral precisely formed. And there was a nice sequence to the numbers, too. A memorable sequence.

An *odd* sequence, he thought as he slid behind the wheel. Maybe it was even a little too rhythmic. *Five-six-seven-eight*…. Wasn't that just a little too handy a combination to be real? It sounded more like an aerobic dance routine than a phone number.

"Was there something you needed to go back

for, dear?" his grandmother asked. "Or are you just planning to sit here and block traffic for the rest of the evening?"

Kurt stared at the ticket still cupped in his palm, and then he reached for his cell phone, angling it in the light from the entrance canopy so he could compare the keypad with what the young woman had written down. The corresponding letters leaped out at him. *Five-six-seven-eight....* He started to laugh.

It looked like a phone number, all right, but he'd bet it led only to a mis-dial recording. Because surely no phone company would deliberately give a customer that particular series of numbers.

The ones which corresponded to the words GET LOST.

Lissa smothered a yawn and tried not to look at the clock posted high on the foyer's opposite wall. The banquet was over, and most of the crowd was gone, but her nerves were still thrumming from the encounter with Kurt Callahan. She couldn't let down her guard yet, however; she had to stay in the cloakroom until the very last garment was claimed or turned over to Lost and Found once the security officers declared that the building was completely empty of guests.

The double doors of the banquet room opened and one of her co-workers emerged pushing a full cart. She looked hot and tired, and Lissa wished she could go lend a hand. Though the work was harder, she'd much rather draw dining room duty than tend the cloakroom. She'd rather be busy than sitting around doing nothing. The time went faster, the tips were usually better, and there was no opportunity to think…

She glanced at the glass tips jar. Not much in it tonight, except for the nice-sized bill Kurt Callahan had pushed through the slot. A big enough bill, in fact, that she half regretted giving him a fake phone number. Not that she would have given him a real one under any circumstances, because Kurt Callahan was the epitome of trouble; she'd learned that lesson long ago. But she could have just told him no.

She hoped he wouldn't actually call. No, she amended, what she really hoped was that the owner of the number wouldn't take offense if he did. She really should have checked out whether that number was actually assigned to a customer…

But then she'd never needed a backup before, because the time and temperature in Winnipeg had served her well through the years. Until tonight— when she'd blurted out the truth to Kurt Callahan. But why had she told him about her ploy? To show off how clever she was? To very delicately let him know that she hadn't been trolling for a date with the athlete? To hint that she needed such stratagems to hold off the vast numbers of men who clustered around her? To point out that even though he wasn't seriously interested in her other men were?

She smothered a snort at her own foolishness. As if any of that would matter to him. A man with his success, and the good looks to match—hair so dark it had had a bluish cast under the artificial lights, blue-gray eyes, a chiseled profile, and a dimple in his cheek which peeked out at the least expected moments—wouldn't have any doubts that he was attractive to any woman still able to breathe.

Maybe she *did* hope he'd call that number. It would do him good to have his ego trimmed back a bit. And if she could be the one to do it… *Somebody has to start a trend,* she thought.

Besides, if she'd coldly refused to give him the information he wanted, he might have started to wonder why. No, this way was better—he wouldn't call, and so he would never have reason to question why the woman in the cloakroom was immune to his charm. He'd probably never give her a second thought.

Her long evening shut up in the cloakroom should have meant plenty of time to finish reviewing her notes for the next morning's political science final. Of course it hadn't quite happened that way. Despite her best efforts, she hadn't been able to concentrate. A dozen times she'd started to study, only to find herself straining to listen to the speeches coming from the ballroom instead.

Well, it was too late to go to the library. She'd

walk straight home instead, look over her notes again, then get some sleep. And once her last exam was past, and she had worked her only remaining dining room shift tomorrow, the semester would officially be over and she would have no other obligations until after January first.

No obligations—but also no income. For with school out of session the student union would close as well.

Lissa bit her lip. She had enough cash tucked back to survive two weeks without a paycheck—and the idea of two weeks of freedom, with no timeclock to punch, no boss to answer to, was sheer heaven.

A crash made her jump and look toward the banquet room. Another of the dining room attendants had misjudged and rammed a cart loaded with the last debris of the banquet—coffee cups, water glasses, crumpled linens, and a few odd baskets of dinner rolls—into the edge of the door. An awkward stack of half-empty glass dessert plates wobbled on the corner of the cart.

Lissa swung herself up onto the cloakroom counter and across, jumping off just as the stack of dishes overbalanced. She slapped her hand down on the top plate, stopping the disaster but splashing leftover creme caramel over the front of her own white shirt and the waitress's. "Sorry about making such a mess, Connie."

"No problem. I'd rather wash out a shirt than

clean glass shards out of the carpet. I think that
stack will stay in place now."

"Now that I've squashed the plates together and
spread dessert all over the foyer, you mean?" Lissa
cautiously lifted her hand. Caramel and custard
oozed between her fingers. "Maybe I should just
lick it off."

"I wouldn't advise it—those things never taste as
good as they look."

Lissa reached for a crumpled napkin and tried
without much success to wipe the sticky sauce off
her fingers.

Their supervisor appeared from the banquet
room. "What's the holdup, girls? And why aren't
you in the cloakroom, Ms Morgan?"

"There are only two coats left, and no one seems
likely to claim them at this hour," Lissa said. "So I
was giving Connie a hand with the cart." She didn't
climb over the counter this time; she very properly
went through the door and back into the cloakroom.

"Connie needs to learn to manage on her own."
The supervisor eyed the glass tip jar. "You seem to
have done rather well this evening. The contribu-
tions of young men, by any chance? Perhaps I
should make it clear, Ms Morgan, that the cloakroom is not a dating service. If I hear again about
you giving out your phone number…."

"Yes, ma'am." Lissa didn't bother to explain.
She suspected her boss would not see the humor in

Winnipeg's time and temperature. And right now she didn't even want to think about how the supervisor might have heard about the whole thing.

"All the guests have gone. Lock up the rest of the coats, and then you may punch out," the supervisor said.

Lissa was relieved to be outside, away from the overheated and stale atmosphere of the banquet room. Now that traffic had died down the snow was getting very deep—though she could see a pair of plows running up the nearest main street, trying to keep the center lanes clear. She slung her backpack over her shoulder, took a deep breath of crisp air, let a snowflake melt on her tongue, and started for home.

Though it was only a few blocks, it took her almost half an hour to struggle through the snow, and by the time she reached the house she was cold and wet. There were still lights on upstairs, but the main level was mercifully dark and relatively quiet. With a sigh of relief she unlocked the sliding door which separated her tiny studio apartment—which in better days had been the back parlor of a once-stately home—from the main hallway.

The fireplace no longer worked, of course, but the mantel served nicely as a display shelf for a few precious objects, and in the center she'd put her Christmas tree. It was just twelve inches tall, the top section of an artificial tree which had been discarded years ago, stuck in a makeshift stand. There were no lights, and only a half-dozen ornaments, each of them really too large for the diminutive tree. But it was a little bit of holiday cheer, a reminder of better days, a symbol of future hopes….

She frowned and looked more closely. There had been a half-dozen ornaments that afternoon, when she'd gone off to work. Now there were five. On the rug below the mantel were a few thin shards of iridescent glass where the sixth ornament, an angel, had shattered.

Someone must have slammed a door, she told herself, and the vibration had made the angel fall. But she knew better. The fact that there were only a few tell-tale slivers meant the ornament had not simply been broken, but the mess had been hastily swept up.

But no one was supposed to be in her room, ever.

Lissa's breath froze. She spun around to the stack of plastic crates which held almost everything she owned and rummaged through the bottom one, looking for her dictionary. In the back of it, under the embroidered cover, was an envelope where she kept her spare cash. She'd tucked it there, secure in the thought that no other occupant of the house would be caught dead looking up a word even if they did invade her privacy to snoop through her room, as she had suspected some of them might be tempted to do.

The envelope was still there, but it was empty. Someone had raided her room, searched her belongings, and walked away with her minuscule savings. All the money she had left in the world now was in her pocket—the tips she'd taken from the glass jar before she left the student union tonight.

She had to remind herself to breathe. Her chest felt as if she was caught between a pair of elevator doors which were squeezing the life out of her.

You've survived hard times before. You can do it again. There would be a check waiting for her when the union reopened after the holidays, pay for the hours she'd worked in the last two weeks.

But in the meantime, to find herself essentially without funds and with no immediate means of earning any….

Maybe, she thought wryly, she should have given Kurt Callahan a real phone number after all. At least then, if by some wild chance he had actually called her, she could have hit him up for a loan, for old times' sake….

By the next afternoon the snowstorm was over, though the wind had picked up. In the residential neighborhood where his grandmother's three-story Dutch Colonial house stood, some of the alleys and sidestreets hadn't yet been plowed. The driveway had been cleared—the handyman had been busy since Kurt had left that morning—but in places small drifts were beginning to form once more, shaped by the wind.

He parked his Jaguar under the porte cochere at the side of the house and went in.

From the kitchen, the scents of warm cinnamon and vanilla swirled around him, mixed with the crisp cold of the outside air. Christmas cookies, he'd bet. He pushed open the swinging shutters which separated the kitchen from the hallway and peered in.

His grandmother's all-purpose household helper was standing on a chair, digging in a top cabinet which looked as if it hadn't been opened in years. As he watched, a stack of odd pans cascaded from the cabinet, raining past Janet's upraised arms and clattering against the hard tile floor.

He offered a hand to help Janet down, and started gathering up pans almost before they'd stopped banging. "Why are you climbing on a chair, anyway? I thought I bought you a ladder for this kind of thing."

"It's in the basement. Too hard to drag it up here. That's the pan I need, the springform one." She took it out of his hand. "Everything else can go back."

If only all of his store managers were as good as Janet at delegating responsibility, Kurt thought, the entire chain would run more smoothly. He gathered up the remaining dozen-odd pans and climbed up on the chair to put them back. "Is Gran home from her lunch date?"

"Not yet. She and Miss Marian always have a lot to talk about."

Including, Kurt remembered ruefully, planning a tea date for him and Marian's "little friend." As if he couldn't see through that for the matchmaking stunt it was. No wonder Gran had been helping to hold off the procession of women at the banquet last night…

"There's fresh coffee," Janet said.

Kurt got himself a cup and carried it and a couple of cookies into the big living room. The sun had come out, and it reflected off the brilliant whiteness outside and poured into the house. The arched panel of leaded glass at the top of the big front window shattered the light into rainbows in which a few dust motes danced like ballerinas.

The enormous fir tree in front of the house swayed in the wind, and a clump of wet snow fell to the sidewalk just as a small reddish car turned the corner and pulled into the driveway. Kurt stared. That was certainly his grandmother's car, but why she would have taken it out in weather like this—

The side door opened and shut, and he met her in the doorway between hall and living room. "What the devil are you doing driving around in this snow?" he demanded.

"The streets are perfectly clear now, dear. We're used to snow in Minneapolis, and the road crews are very good at their job."

"It's freezing out there, Gran. The wind chill must be—"

"A man who climbs mountains for fun is worried about wind chill?"

"Not for myself," he growled. "For you. You

could get stranded. You could have a fender-bender. Just last night you were telling me how much you appreciated having a good, reliable driver."

"Very true. It's quite a fine idea, in fact. Would you hang up my coat, dear? And ask Janet to brew a pot of tea." She dropped her mink carelessly on the floor and walked into the living room.

Kurt bit his tongue and started for the kitchen. Just as he pushed open the swinging shutters to call to Janet the side door opened again, and he had to jerk back to prevent his toes from being caught under the edge. Cold wind swirled in, and a feminine voice called, "Mrs. Wilder?"

"I'm just across the hall," his grandmother answered from the living room. "Come on in."

A face appeared around the edge of the door. A heart-shaped face with very short auburn hair ruffled around the ears and cheeks reddened by the wind. The young woman from the cloakroom.

Kurt stared at her in disbelief. "Where did you come from?"

She didn't answer directly. "I didn't expect you to be here. I mean—right here. I didn't bang the door into your nose, did I?"

Finally things clicked. What was wrong with him that it had taken so long to make the connection? "I should have known Marian's 'little friend' would turn out to be you," he grumbled. No wonder she'd looked at him that way last night. She'd been speculating, all right—wondering what his reaction would be when he finally figured out who she was. "Is that why you pulled all that nonsense with the phone number last night? So I'd be surprised when you turned up here?"

She flushed suddenly, violently red. "Look, I'm sorry about the phone number. It was a stupid trick, and if someone took it as a prank call—"

"I didn't have to dial it to figure out the joke."

"You didn't? Then I honestly don't know what you're talking about. All I did was drive your grandmother home from the student union."

He rubbed the stubble on his chin. "Why?"

His grandmother crossed the hall to the stairs. "Kurt, you said yourself just now that I shouldn't be driving in weather like this, so Lissa drove me home." Her voice faded as she reached the top of the staircase.

Kurt stared at the young woman again. "You're *not* the friend of Marian's that Gran invited to tea?"

She shook her head. "Sorry to disappoint you. Are you talking about Marian Meadows? I know who she is, but that's all."

"Then what are you doing here?"

"I'm trying to tell you, if you'll just listen. Actually, I'm glad to find that you haven't gone back to Seattle yet."

"You've done your homework, I see. Not that it's hard to find out where I live."

Her gaze flickered, and he felt a flash of satisfaction at disconcerting her. But she didn't explain, or defend herself. "Maybe you can convince your grandmother to see a doctor," she went on. "I didn't get anywhere when I tried."

His attention snapped back to her like a slingshot. "Doctor?"

"She had a dizzy spell. She'd had lunch at the restaurant in the student union. Mrs. Meadows left, and Hannah—"

"You're on a first-name basis?"

"Your grandmother stayed to finish her coffee. When she stood up, she almost passed out. I tried to get her to go to the emergency room, but she insisted she was fine to come home."

"So you grabbed the opportunity to drive her out here."

"She was going to drive herself," the young woman protested.

"Why not just put her in a cab?"

"She didn't want to leave her car there to be towed by the snowplow crews. Will you quit yelling at me and think about it? I'm betting that's just like her."

She was right, Kurt admitted. His grandmother was perfectly capable of refusing to see a doctor, and of insisting on not leaving her car unattended, of driving when she shouldn't. And she was behaving oddly—she didn't normally fling her coat onto the floor.

"Thank you for bringing her home," he said quietly. "I'll take it from here."

But the woman didn't budge. She looked almost uncomfortable.

Kurt wondered why she didn't just go. Was she waiting for some sort of payment? Or did she have something else on her mind?

He frowned as he remembered the flash of familiarity he'd felt last night. He'd dismissed that as the look of a woman on the prowl. But had it been more than that? He tipped his head to one side and looked closely. Tall, slim and straight, red hair and big brown eyes, and a smile full of magic… What had his grandmother called her?

A few random words swirled in his brain and settled into a pattern. *Magic smile. Lissa. You've done your homework….*

"Calculus class," he said softly. "You're Lissa Morgan."

It was no wonder, really, that he hadn't recognized her last night. There was nothing about this slender, vivid woman with the huge brown eyes which even resembled the lanky, awkward girl who was stored in his memory—the one with frizzy carrot-colored hair straggling to the middle of her back. The freshman frump, some of his fellow students had called her—dressed in oversized shapeless sweaters and with her face always buried in a math book.

And yet there was one thing which hadn't changed. He'd seen it last night when she'd smiled, and that was why she'd looked familiar, despite all the surface changes. Because the only other time that she'd ever smiled at him....

That was long ago, he told himself. *Another lifetime, in fact.*

Still, no wonder he'd been itchy around her last night. No wonder he'd picked at her, egged her on, found fault with everything she did. His subconscious mind must have recognized her, despite all the changes in her looks.

"So you're still hanging around the university?" he said. "I figured by now you'd be head actuary for some big pension fund or insurance company or national bank. Or an engineer somewhere in the space program. Or—no, I have it. You must be working undercover at the student union, checking for fraud. Because I'm sure a woman with the brainpower you've got would never be satisfied with just running a cloakroom."

Her jaw tightened, and he thought for a second she was going to take a swing at him.

"She's not running a cloakroom," his grandmother said from the stairway landing. "Not anymore. Kurt, Lissa is my new driver. Only I'm going to call her my personal assistant, because it sounds so much nicer. Don't you agree?"

CHAPTER TWO

IF HANNAH WILDER had pulled the stair railing loose and hit her grandson over the head with it, Kurt couldn't have looked more dazed. Under other circumstances, Lissa thought, she might have enjoyed watching him turn green. She wondered whether it was Hannah's announcement or his past coming back to haunt him which had caused Kurt's reaction.

Then she almost snorted at the idea. As if Lissa Morgan popping back into his life after all this time could have any such stunning effect on him. Frankly, she was surprised that even her name had jolted his memory loose. Any guy who would make a bet with his buddies on whether he could get the most unpopular girl in the class to believe that he was interested in her—and prove it in the most intimate of ways—just so they could all laugh at her for the rest of the semester because she'd been taken in by his charm, wouldn't bother to remember the details six years later.

Unless she'd been an even funnier joke to him than she'd realized. Unless she'd been an even easier conquest than he'd hoped for.

Which, of course, she had been. Stupid—that was the only word for her back then.

He'd been a senior in college, taking advanced math for the second time to fill out his requirements, struggling to get his grade point far enough above the danger level so he could graduate in a couple of months. So when he'd asked her—only a freshman, but the most advanced student in the class nevertheless—to tutor him, there had been no reason for Lissa to think he might not be telling the truth about his motives....

Stop it, she thought. That was all over. Her days as the frump were long past. If anything, she should thank Kurt Callahan, because in a convoluted way he'd inspired her to lose the frizzy hair and the bulky sweaters and make herself into an entirely new woman....

Yeah, right, she thought dryly. *Keep talking, Lissa, and maybe you'll convince yourself that a one-night stand with him was a good thing.*

Still, she wasn't about to let herself overreact now; she was bigger than that, and running into him again wasn't going to change anything.

So what if he was even better-looking now than he'd been in college, with his crisp black hair and unusual blue-gray eyes, his youthful arrogance mellowed by time and success into something more like self-confidence? It didn't matter to her anymore.

But why couldn't that encounter last night have been the end of it? She'd been proud of the way she'd handled herself in the cloakroom standoff. She hadn't lost her temper or embarrassed herself. She hadn't even needed to publicly rub his nose in the facts in order to feel good about telling him to get lost. But now that she was face to face with him once more…. Now that he had remembered her….

Hannah's offer had seemed so simple on the drive from the student union to her house. And it was so perfectly logical. *You need a job,* Hannah had said. *And I need some help for a while. We can be a team.* What difference did it make whether the woman offering to hire her was Kurt Callahan's grandmother? He wouldn't know anything about it.

Only here he was—in the flesh. And what nice flesh it was, too, Lissa thought. Today he wasn't wearing a suit, but khakis and a polo shirt, and the clothing showed him off nicely. He was tanned and athletic without being showy—no overdone bulges of biceps. In fact, he was perfectly proportioned, without a flaw anywhere to draw the eye. He might be a little more muscular than he'd been six years ago, a little more imposing. But even then he'd been pretty much perfect—strong and hard and clean and intoxicatingly attractive.

In short, she admitted, he'd been simply intoxicating. He'd acted on her senses like a rich old brandy, sweeping away every inhibition, every fragment of common sense…. He'd used his charm, he'd used *her*, just so he could win a bet.

What a shame it was that Kurt Callahan's flaws were on the inside. He hadn't had a conscience six years ago, and she doubted very much that he'd grown one since.

Well, she'd just have to work around him, that was all. Surely he wouldn't be staying in Minneapolis for long—a man with his responsibilities? And Hannah's plan was not only simple, logical and sensible, it was the best deal Lissa was likely to find.

How it had come about, however, was nothing short of fantastic, when Lissa stopped to think about it. She'd simply been doing her job, taking care of two elderly lunch patrons. She'd seen them many times before in the union's dining room—they were simply Mrs. Wilder and Mrs. Meadows, and she treated them as she did every other patron.

Then Mrs. Meadows had left, and Hannah Wilder had sat still a little longer, drinking her coffee and chatting as Lissa cleared the table and brought her receipt. And then she'd got up from her chair, reeled, and almost fallen….

Lissa still didn't quite understand why she'd actually told Hannah about the money which was missing from her room. More than twelve hours after the discovery she'd still been a bit dazed over the realization that she'd been robbed, of course. But why she'd actually confided in Hannah—who had enough problems of her own just then—was beyond her.

However, Hannah had asked her to sit down for a few minutes and keep her company while she recovered from her spell of lightheadedness. And then she'd looked straight into Lissa's eyes and said, "What's troubling you, my dear?"

It was the first time in months that anyone had treated Lissa with such obvious personal concern. One thing had led to another, the words had come tumbling out…and here she was.

"Driver?" Kurt said.

Lissa pulled herself back to the moment.

"Personal assistant," Hannah corrected. She came down the last few stairs, holding tightly to the railing. "If you insist on discussing it, Kurt, let's go back into the living room and have a seat."

Kurt was instantly beside her, offering an arm. "I'm sorry, Gran—I forgot you weren't feeling well."

"It was only a momentary weak spell, and it has passed. I got up too suddenly, that's all. I'm certainly not an invalid."

Lissa couldn't stop herself. "But if your blood pressure is likely to behave like a jumping jack, you shouldn't be driving."

Kurt shot a look at Lissa. "I can't disagree with that—though it sounds self-serving when it's *you* who's saying it. I suppose you're the one who suggested the whole plan?"

"The only thing she suggested was that I see a doctor," Hannah said placidly. "I don't think the idea of a driver would have occurred to Lissa at all. Since she doesn't have a car herself, she doesn't think in those terms."

Kurt was starting to look like a thundercloud. "You don't have a car? Do you even have a driver's license?"

"All students do," Hannah put in. "I understand there's some rule about not being able to go into a bar without one."

You're not helping matters, Hannah. Lissa put her chin up and looked squarely at Kurt. "I have a perfectly valid driver's license, and not just to use as proof of my age so I can go out drinking."

"When's the last time you were behind the wheel of a car?"

She'd been hoping he wouldn't ask that. "I suppose you mean before today? A while."

His eyes narrowed.

"All right, it's been—maybe three years. I don't remember."

"Great. Add up the two of you, and we still have a mediocre, inexperienced driver."

Much as she wanted to, Lissa couldn't exactly argue with that. Between the unfamiliar car and the slick streets she'd been nervous, on edge, and too cautious for their own good, creeping along at a snail's pace in fear of losing control. But at least she knew her limitations.

"They say you never forget how," Hannah added helpfully. "Or were they talking about bicycles?"

Kurt rubbed the back of his neck. "Gran, it's a wonderful idea for you not to drive anymore. But since Janet doesn't drive either, it would be much better to sell the car and use the money for taxis. The car's probably only worth a few hundred dollars, but that's a lot of taxi rides."

With all his money, Lissa thought, he could buy Hannah her own private limo service. Instead he was suggesting she sell her car and tuck the money away in a taxi fund? "I didn't realize you had such a cheap streak, Kurt."

He shot a look at her. "I'm not the one with the cheap streak."

"I hate to wait for a ride," Hannah said. "In fact, I hate taxis all the way around—they smell. And a cabby won't walk you into a doctor's office."

"That's why you have Janet."

"Janet's no steadier on her feet than I am these days." Hannah laughed lightly. "You should have seen us trying to buff the hardwood floor in your room before you came, Kurt—we must have looked like the Three Stooges on ice. Well, two of them, at least."

"Why were you buffing…?" Kurt closed his eyes

as if he were in pain. "Never mind. How often do you even leave the house?"

Hannah began ticking points off on her fingertips. "The hairdresser, the massage clinic, physical therapy, the doctor, the pharmacy, the grocery store, the bank, my broker, the—"

"All right, I take your point. What about a limo service? They don't smell."

"I'd still have to wait around for someone to come and pick me up. And it would be expensive, because I go out at least once a day. I deliberately split up my errands and appointments so that every day I get some fresh air and exercise."

"I can afford it, Gran."

"Waste is waste, no matter who's paying for it."

Kurt shot a look at Lissa. "See? I told you I'm not the one with the cheap streak."

"I'm not cheap," Hannah said. "I just like to get value for money. So if you're worried about Lissa getting off too easily, don't. She'll have plenty to keep her occupied, helping me out."

"Gran, you can't have it both ways. If you're saying now that you're ill enough to need someone right beside you all the time, then surely a personal nurse would be a better choice?"

"Oh, no." Hannah took a deep breath and let her gaze wander around the room, as if she'd rather look anywhere than at him. "I don't need a nurse. Just an extra pair of hands and a strong set of legs.

I wasn't going to break the news to you just yet, Kurt, but I suppose it's time to tell you."

Here it comes, Lissa thought. She hadn't quite believed it herself when Hannah had told her. Not that it was any of her business, but she felt like ducking behind the couch to avoid the worst of the explosion when Kurt heard the news.

"Tell me what?" Kurt sounded wary. Almost fearful.

"I've decided to give up the house," Hannah said simply. "I'm just not up to taking care of it anymore, and neither is Janet."

"Then hire a housekeeping service."

Despite her best efforts, Lissa couldn't keep her mouth shut. "Perhaps you could stop snapping out orders and just listen for a change?"

Hannah was smiling. "Thank you, Lissa dear. It's really no wonder that the women he dates have such a short shelf-life, is it? I can't blame them for getting tired of it."

"I'm only trying to help!" Kurt's voice was almost a bark.

"In such a typically masculine way, too," Hannah murmured. "Your grandfather used to do the same thing—as soon as I complained about something he would tell me precisely how I should solve the problem. It was really quite annoying, and I never managed to break him of it... At any rate, I have a housekeeping service already. It's not the work I'm concerned about, Kurt, it's the responsibility."

Kurt frowned.

"I'm tired of writing out a list for the housecleaning team and making sure they follow it. I want someone else to think about the weeds in the flowerbeds and the leaves in the gutters, and whether the draperies in the guestroom need to be replaced or just taken down and sent along to the cleaners."

Kurt rubbed his finger along the bridge of his nose. "I see. You're talking about moving into some kind of retirement community, I suppose, where they do all that stuff for you? I'll see what's available, and—"

"You mean you'll assign someone on your staff to see what's available? Anyway, I've already looked. I know where I want to go. It's a very nice apartment complex which provides all the assistance anyone could want—and doesn't bother people when they don't want help."

Kurt shrugged. "All right, Gran. Whatever you want to do."

The gesture looked as if it hurt him, Lissa thought. Clearly this was a man who didn't enjoy being left out of the loop.

"When are you planning to do this?"

"Well, that's a bit more difficult. I can't just lock the door and walk off. This house holds many years of memories to be sorted out, and only I can do that. But Lissa's going to be my hands and feet while I get the job done—starting tomorrow. I'm going to go upstairs for a nap now, so you just entertain yourselves for a while, children."

As her footsteps retreated up the stairs, Kurt turned to Lissa. "If you think you're going to walk in here and get away with this—"

It was clearly time to take a stand. "Get away with what? I'd say Hannah's the boss, and you're not—so what she decides goes, Kurt."

"Maybe I can't contradict her orders. But I can darned sure try to make sure she's safe. Put your coat on."

"Why?"

"Well, we're not going to go build a snowman. Before I let you start chauffeuring Gran around, you're going to have to pass a driving test. Scare me, and you flunk. Got it?"

She would have told him to jump headfirst into a snowdrift, except that Lissa knew some practice behind the wheel would be a very good idea—and she figured if she could drive safely with a frustrated Kurt riding shotgun, then she wouldn't be putting Hannah into any danger at all. And if his backseat driving got to be unbearable, she mused, she would just slam the passenger side of the car into a tree somewhere and walk home....

"Watch out for that truck," Kurt said, and Lissa pulled her attention back to the street.

Hannah's car was small and light, and as the afternoon waned and traffic grew heavier the packed-down snow which remained on the streets grew ever more slippery. But, after a false start or two, Lissa's confidence began to come back, despite the silent and glowering male in the passenger seat next to her.

Maybe Hannah had been right after all, she thought, and driving a car—like riding a bicycle—was a skill which never quite vanished from the subconscious mind. If it didn't bother her to have Kurt either issuing instructions or seething not quite silently—like a pasta pot just about to boil—then she could handle normal traffic along with Hannah's chatter with no trouble at all.

"Well?" she said finally, after a solid hour of negotiating everything from narrow alleys to eight-lane freeways. "Since I haven't smashed either you or the car, and you haven't grabbed for the steering wheel or the brake in at least twenty minutes, I'm going to assume that the test is over and take you back to Hannah's house."

"Not quite. Parallel park in front of that diner up there."

"Parallel park? Nobody ever has to actually *do* that."

His level look said that she would do it or else, so Lissa sighed and took a stab at it. Two tries later she was quite proud of the result. "Good enough?"

"Shut the car off. Let's have a cup of coffee."

"I'm honored at the invitation, but—"

"Don't be. This is the only way we can talk without Gran interrupting."

"We've been riding around for an hour," Lissa protested, "and you haven't had a word to say the whole time. So why should I—?"

"I wasn't going to risk taking your attention off the road. Come on." He slammed the car door and kicked at the wad of snow and ice which had built up behind the front wheel. "Looks like this thing could stand some new tires. Would you like coffee, tea, or hot chocolate?"

She settled for tea and refused a piece of apple pie to go with it. Kurt surveyed her over the rim of his coffee cup and said, "All right, what's really going on here? How did all this happen?"

Lissa sighed. "I didn't stalk your grandmother, if that's what you're suggesting. It just happened to be my table she chose at lunchtime. There aren't all that many of us working at the union, you know—not as regulars in the dining room, at least. It's also the last day before the holidays, so a lot of the kids who work there have already gone home for Christmas."

She waited for him to ask why she wasn't going anywhere for Christmas. But he didn't.

"Look," Lissa said, "I'll tell you exactly what happened. Mrs. Meadows left because she had an appointment of some sort, and your grandmother stayed to finish her coffee. I cleared the dessert dishes, she wished me a Merry Christmas, then she got up from the table and started to sway. I helped her back in her chair and offered to find a doctor. She said no, but would I just sit down with her for a minute, so I did. Then when she felt better she asked if I'd walk her out to her car. When I found out she was planning to drive herself home, I suggested she take a cab, and—"

"And she offered you a job? Just like that?"

"She's not quite that fast a worker," Lissa admitted. "It took her maybe ten minutes in all."

"Why?"

"Ask her. How should I know why she offered me a job?"

"I will. But what I really want to know is why you took it."

"Because I need a job—"

"But *why* do you need a job? You were the math whiz of the entire campus—why aren't you a chief financial officer at some big corporation by now?"

All the plans she had made and the dreams she had dreamed…. Lissa had thought she'd come to terms with all the losses and the delays, but it wasn't until now—when Kurt Callahan asked the question in that slightly cynical tone—that she realized how much it hurt that after so long she was still marking time.

"Did you get caught with your fingers in the till, or what?"

Lissa bristled. "No. I'm still here because I had

to drop out for a while. I have one more semester to go before I finish my degree."

He went absolutely still. "Why, Lissa?"

"Why should it matter to you? It's long over with." Then she bit her lip and said quietly, "I'm still here because my father got lymphoma and I had to drop out and take care of him in the last year of his life. That cost me my scholarships, because walking out in the middle of a term doesn't sit well with the financial aid people around here. I worked for a while, and saved money to come back, but I was just getting up to speed again when I got pneumonia. That knocked me down for months. I couldn't keep up with classes, so I had to quit again."

He seemed to be waiting for something else. Finally, when the silence drew out painfully, he said, "That's nasty luck."

Was there a hidden meaning in his tone? She told herself it was pointless to try to analyze. "Yes, it was."

"But hardly anything new for you. You dropped out of that calculus class, too."

"Noticed that, did you?" Lissa said dryly. "I'm amazed you were paying attention."

"Dammit, Lissa, I tried to talk to you, but you wouldn't listen. You wouldn't even stop walking down the hall, much less let me apologize. And then before I knew it you were gone—"

"So what would you have said you were sorry for? Not making love, I'll bet."

"No," he admitted. "Not that."

"Then what? Getting caught? Making sure everybody in the class knew you'd won your bet?" She saw curiosity flicker in his eyes, and she took a deep breath and reminded herself that it didn't matter anymore. The last thing she wanted to do was let him think she still cared. She'd buried those feelings long ago. "One-night stands happen, Kurt. I was quite a little more innocent than you were, that's true, and it annoyed the hell out of me that you'd told everyone in class I slept with you—"

"I didn't tell them."

"Oh, really? Then how did they know? I don't recall them being in your room observing."

A smile tugged at the corner of his mouth. "Lissa, a brass band could have marched through my room that night and you wouldn't have noticed."

Heat swept up her throat, over her face. "The point is, it's over. There's nothing to be gained by dissecting what happened." *Though at the time I'd have liked to dissect you.* "I believe, before we got sidetracked a few minutes ago, that you were asking why I need a second job. Right now my budget's unusually tight, so—"

"Couldn't you make more at some other kind of job, instead of working at the union?"

"Possibly. But waiting tables isn't a bad income, really. Most of our clients are alumni, and the tips are usually generous. Besides, the hours are flexible, and I don't have to waste any time commuting. I can work an hour here and there and fit partial shifts in between classes. If I had to go all the way across town to a job I wouldn't make any more, even if I got a higher rate of pay for each hour I worked."

"Because it would take so long to get there, especially since you don't have a car. I see. Still, I wouldn't think you'd have gotten in over your head financially, wizard with figures that you are."

"It's hard to pay tuition and medical bills at the same time. Pneumonia's not cheap, and I didn't have any health insurance after my dad died."

"Perhaps some financial planning advice—"

"There you go, problem-solving again. I'm sure your banker would be tickled pink to handle my portfolio, because I've usually got about fifty bucks to my name." She was irritated enough not to stop and think before she went on. "I'd saved up enough to get through a couple of weeks with no income— but then I was robbed last night."

His eyebrows went up. "Are you all right?"

"Oh, yes—thanks for asking. I wasn't held up at gunpoint or anything. I'd left my extra funds in my room—only I obviously didn't pick a good enough hiding spot." She knew she sounded bitter, and probably stupid, too. She waited for him to say it.

He didn't. "Did you call the police?"

"No. It wouldn't do much good. It was cash, and there's no way to prove that any specific twenty-dollar bill was mine once. Besides, if I'm right about my suspicions, and the thief *is* someone else who lives in the house—"

"You think your roommate robbed you?"

Why had she told him anything at all? Of course it had seemed safe, because he'd never been known for tenacity back in their college days. Quite the opposite, in fact—at least when it came to studying. But now he seemed to be like a bulldog with a bone, and it was too late to back out without explanation. "We're not what you'd call roommates," Lissa said reluctantly. "Or even housemates, for that matter. It's more like a boarding house. Seven individual bedrooms, shared kitchen and bath. Reporting it would only make things more difficult in the future. Nothing would be safe."

He nodded. "You always were pragmatic."

"You don't have to make it sound like a disease. In some situations there aren't any good choices, Kurt. You just deal with it and go on, that's all."

He didn't answer, but he pushed his apple pie away as if he'd lost his appetite.

Puzzled at the response, Lissa went on. "Anyway, to get back to the point—your grandmother got that much out of me and then she went all quiet. The next thing I knew—"

"She'd manufactured a job for you."

"You mean she made it up from nothing? I don't think so. If she's going to move out of that house, she really does need help. There must be closets everywhere. Unless you're planning to stick around to pack boxes…?"

Kurt gave a little shiver.

Lissa went on coolly, "Yeah, what a surprise. You're too busy, right?"

"I'll hire a crew."

"She doesn't want a crew, she wants me."

"Maybe she thinks she does—right now."

"And what does that mean? If you're threatening to discredit me by telling her what happened between us all those years ago I suggest you think again, because you won't exactly come off as Mr. Pure of Heart yourself. Anyway, someone will have to do the work, so why shouldn't it be me?"

"How long do you think it will take?"

"I have two weeks free until school starts up again."

"Surely you don't think that job can be done in two weeks? And if you start dragging things out of dark closets and then abandon her—"

"Hello? What was that you were telling your grandmother earlier about not being able to have things both ways? Neither can you, fella. At any rate, I figure within two weeks Hannah will either have decided that she's too fond of her house to leave it, or she'll have gotten tired of sorting and decided to call an auctioneer and get it over with in a hurry."

He stared at her as if he were seeing her for the

first time. "So in the meantime you're just going to let her pay you for humoring her?"

"I intend to do whatever she asks me to. You know, it might not be a bad plan for you to follow, too. Humoring her, I mean, instead of arguing with her all the time." *And maybe you could see your way clear to cutting me a little slack, too.* She'd probably better not hold her breath, though.

She looked at her watch. "I don't mean to rush you, Kurt, but I have things to do. And, since your hair hasn't turned white yet, I'm going to assume I passed the driving test."

"We're not all the way home yet. And I'm in no hurry to get back in that car. I felt like I was riding around in a tomato soup can."

"Well, it's not my fault that your grandmother drives a compact. If you're used to the Jaguar I saw parked outside the house—"

"Don't even daydream about driving my car. Buy her some new tires first thing, all right? Give me the bill for them." He stood up and pulled out his wallet.

Lissa sat very still, her tea mug clutched between her hands. "Then you're withdrawing your objections?"

"No. But since she seems set on the idea, I'm putting my objections on hold."

At least he wasn't still threatening her. Quite sensible of him, she thought. "Fair enough." Once back in the car, she turned on the radio and hummed along with Christmas carols as she drove. She thought Kurt was looking even more like an approaching rainstorm. "What's the matter?" she asked finally. "You don't like 'Jingle Bells'?"

"Not when it's played on accordion and banjo, thanks. Where did you find that station?"

"I didn't choose it, it was already tuned in. Why doesn't your grandmother have a Christmas tree?"

"Tradition. It goes up one week before Christmas."

Lissa calculated. "That's tomorrow."

"Enjoy the job," Kurt said. "I'd help, but I'll be at the grand opening of my new Twin Cities store."

"Oh, that's what's keeping you here." Lissa parked the car right behind the Jaguar, under the porte cochere.

"The grand opening runs through the weekend." Kurt walked around to her side and opened her door. "Aren't you coming in?"

"No, I'm just dropping you off."

"Wait a minute. You're taking Gran's car? Do the words grand theft auto mean anything to you?"

She looked out over the dull red finish on the car's hood. "Not *grand* theft, surely? Now, if I was taking *your* car, then I could understand you saying—" He started to growl, and Lissa thought better of pursuing the argument. "She told me I could."

"You're planning to commute using Gran's car? And what other employee benefits have you talked her into providing?"

"Not to commute, exactly." Her gloved hands tightened on the wheel, and she looked up at him through her lashes, waiting to enjoy the explosion she expected. "I'm just taking it today so I can load up my stuff." She paused for just a second to let the news sink in, then added gently, "And of course I need to talk to my landlady as well—to give notice that I'm moving in with Hannah."

And before he could open his mouth Lissa put the car in reverse and backed out into the street.

The sense of freedom was incredible. Traffic on the outbound streets was a disaster, but nobody was trying to get downtown this late in the day, and the little car buzzed along easily. For the first time in years Lissa wasn't simply enduring Christmas carols, she was enjoying them. With the dim prospect of two weeks of living on macaroni and noodles now erased from her calendar, life was definitely looking up.

Of course there was the little matter of Kurt Callahan lurking in the background. But once his grand opening was past he'd be going home, and that interference would be gone as well. With him out of the way her peace of mind would be restored, and she and Hannah could get down to some serious digging and sorting...for a while, at least.

The nerve of the man, threatening to tell Hannah what had happened between them all those years ago. Of course he wouldn't actually do it, because *he'd* be the one who ended up looking bad. Still….

Lissa had thought she was long over the sting of the single evening she'd spent with him. Even in the cloakroom last night she hadn't entirely lost her perspective. But that had been before she'd had to deal with him on such a personal level, and now all the feelings had come flashing back: the frustration and the anger, the hurt, the desolation and—yes, the attraction too. Because he *had* been attractive, even to a frump of a freshman who'd known perfectly well that he was far beyond her sphere. A *dumb* frump of a freshman, Lissa reminded herself, who had bought the tale of his needing tutoring—which had certainly been true, as far as it went—and who had gotten in way over her head. And only when it had been too late had she found out that the whole thing had been the result of a bet, with the entire class in on it. That the single night which had been so magical to her had meant less than nothing to him.

You dropped out of that calculus class, too, he'd said.

Well, he was almost right. She'd stuck it out for a while, hoping it would all blow over and everybody would forget that stupid bet. But though the professor had kept order in the classroom, the teasing before and after class hadn't ceased. After a while she'd made herself so sick over it that she'd skipped the rest of the lectures and turned in her work at the professor's office. Only the fact that she was such a promising student had kept her from finishing up with a failing grade.

Just one more thing that Kurt Callahan was responsible for....

The steps up to the front of the boarding house were still buried in eight inches of snow, though a couple of trails had been broken by people going in and out. Lissa picked her way carefully up to the porch and let herself into the hallway. The landlady was standing outside the room which had originally been the front parlor, arguing with the tenant who was supposed to pay part of his rent by shoveling the walks.

Lissa unlocked her own door, then cleared her throat.

The landlady turned her head. "What do you want?"

Lissa debated. It wasn't smart to announce that her room would be unoccupied for a while—but she couldn't simply disappear for two weeks without letting the landlady know, either. "I just wanted to let you know that I'm going away for a while."

The woman looked at her suspiciously. "How long a while? You going to pay for January in advance?"

Lissa couldn't pay in advance if she wanted to. Not on the proceeds of last night's tips. "I'll pay for January when January comes," she said firmly. "Just as I do every month."

The front door opened again, and she saw the landlady's eyes widen as she spotted the newcomer. Lissa looked around to see who had come in, and her heart sank.

CHAPTER THREE

KURT STAMPED HIS feet on the doormat and cast a long look around the dim hallway of the boarding house. The wallpaper was peeling, the glass in the door rattled as he closed it, the floorboards creaked under his feet, and the air smelled of burned popcorn.

Lissa looked over her shoulder. "Fancy meeting you here. I suppose Hannah gave you the address?"

"She sent me over to help so you'd be finished moving in time for dinner."

The landlady stopped yelling and bustled over. "Did you say you're moving?"

"I'm not giving up the room," Lissa said. "I'm just picking up the stuff I'll need for a couple of weeks."

The landlady folded her arms across her ample chest. "If you want me to hold the room, you'll have to pay ahead of time for January. Otherwise, how do I know you'll come back?"

Kurt stepped between them. "You trust her—the

same way she trusts you not to put the rest of her stuff out on the curb the minute her back is turned."

The landlady gave him the same stare she would a bedbug and went on, "And don't expect me to return your deposit if you do give up the room, because there's a hole in the wall." She returned to the front parlor and went back to haranguing the other tenant.

"Home sweet home," Lissa said. "The hole in the wall was there when I moved in."

Honestly curious, Kurt asked, "Why do you put up with this?"

"Because it isn't for much longer, and because living cheaply now means I won't have so much debt to pay after I get my degree."

"But you can't want to come back here, after you were robbed."

"Well, that's rather beside the point, isn't it?" Lissa pushed a door open. The sliding panel squeaked and stuck, and she gave it an extra shove.

In some situations there aren't any good choices, she had said. *You deal with it and go on.*

It was starting to look to him like she was an expert at dealing with things and going on. Nursing a sick father, getting pneumonia herself....

She'd had a streak of hard luck, there was no doubt about that, but he couldn't help but wonder if there was even more to the story than she'd told him.

Kurt followed her in. She flipped on every light

in the place—such as they were. How she managed to get dressed in this gloom, much less read or study, was beyond him.

His gaze came to rest on the mantel, where a little Christmas tree stood bravely in the center, drooping under the weight of five too-big ornaments.

Damn. He didn't want to feel sorry for her... but he did.

"You pack," he said. "I'll carry."

The trouble was, Lissa had no idea what to pack. Clothes weren't a problem—her wardrobe was limited, so she figured she'd just pile everything into a crate and take it along. It was all the other things she wasn't sure about.

All the other things. What an all-encompassing, grandiose statement that was, Lissa told herself, considering how few material goods she actually possessed. Everything she owned would fit in the back of a minivan with room to spare.

Kurt came back from his third trip out to the car and raised an eyebrow at the half-empty crate Lissa was contemplating. "What's the holdup?"

"I'm trying to decide what else to take."

He looked around, as if he had no idea what she could be talking about.

She had to give him a little credit, though—Kurt hadn't said a single disparaging word about her surroundings, her belongings, or the fact that her luggage consisted of plastic crates and not the mono-grammed leather bags his crowd probably carried.

"Besides clothes, what could you possibly need?"

"Books, maybe. I wonder if I'll have time to start studying for my spring classes."

"Those would be the classes that won't start until January? You already have the books?"

"Some of them. Picking up one or two at a time is easier on the wallet than buying them all at once."

He looked startled, as if he'd never thought of that before.

His expression made it perfectly obvious, Lissa thought, that budgeting for textbooks had never been a problem for Kurt Callahan. "It's sort of like putting money in the bank," she said. "Buying what you need ahead of time, I mean."

"So if you had invested all your cash in math books rather than just leaving it lying around, you wouldn't be in this spot."

"It wasn't lying around, it was hidden." *Just not well enough.* "And if I'd bought all my books with it I'd still have had a problem—namely, what I was going to eat for the next two weeks."

"Speaking of eating," Kurt suggested, "Janet promised prime rib for dinner, and I like mine rare. So can we hurry this project along?"

Lissa's stomach growled at the mere suggestion of rare prime rib. Or, for that matter, medium or well-done prime rib; it didn't matter, because it all sounded the same to her. Delicious, in a word.

"Just grab everything you might need, and let's go."

"Everything?" she said doubtfully.

"Sure. That's really what's bothering you, isn't it? You're wondering if the vandals around here will pop in to inspect whatever you've left behind and destroy it if it isn't of any value to them."

She couldn't argue with that, since it was exactly what she'd been thinking. It was the reason she'd hesitated to tell the landlady that she'd be gone at all. If word got around that she wouldn't be back for a couple of weeks she might as well leave the door standing wide open.

Still, her pride was nicked at the idea of dragging out the detritus of her life in front of him.

In front of *anyone,* she corrected herself. It wasn't specifically Kurt she was sensitive about. She didn't like letting anyone see the pathetically few sentimental things that remained to her.

Kurt strolled over to the mantel and picked up a textbook from the political science class she'd just finished. "What are you taking next semester?"

He was actually trying to make things easier for her—making conversation to cover her discomfort. If she had half a brain, Lissa thought, she'd be grateful. Instead, she was unreasonably annoyed— as if he'd come right out and said that he realized she had reason to be embarrassed, so he would do the proper etiquette thing and pretend not to notice. As if etiquette and good behavior were a big consideration with him!

She gathered up a couple of bags of books and kept her voice level. "Accounting theory, auditing, organizing information systems, advanced database programming—"

"What do you do for a hobby? Write the computer code for the federal government to calculate income tax?"

"I could," Lissa said calmly. "In fact, I have. Not the government's software, but a sample package for a small corporation. That was last year, in my tax practicum." She pulled a ragged box from under the bed.

Kurt ran a hand over the back of his neck. "I'm curious—do the words *pizza and a movie* mean anything to you? You notice I'm not even talking about anything as elaborate as going to a basketball game or a dance."

She shrugged. "I don't have the time or money for entertainment."

"Everybody needs to relax. And you can't tell me those guys hanging around the cloakroom last night wouldn't buy you a pizza. That looks like a very old quilt."

"Congratulations, you win a prize." She shook

her head and started to push it back. "Nobody would steal that."

"What is it, honestly. Your security blanket?" He took the box out of her hands. "If it's really old, somebody might just pick it up. Better take it."

"Hannah's got enough of her own old stuff to deal with."

"It's a big guestroom. She and Janet are probably getting it ready for you right now, putting in all the little touches to make it feel like home. You know, scented towels, fresh flowers, robe and slippers laid out, a chocolate mint on the pillow…."

Lissa looked around the drab little room. "That *will* make it feel just like home," she said dryly. "And in case you're trying to hurry me along by pointing out that I'm supposed to be relieving Hannah of household duties, not creating more work for her—"

"The idea had crossed my mind."

"Yes, and I already feel guilty about being here instead of helping out. But so should you—I caught what she said about waxing the floor for you." She got her single good dress from the closet and folded it carefully atop a crate. "Why aren't you already in the guestroom, anyway?"

"Because she keeps it for guests," Kurt explained, with an air of long-suffering patience. "She always has. I have my own room up on the top floor, reserved from the time when I was a kid and went to visit her for the summers."

"Every year? You mean, like all summer?"

"Yeah."

"And she put you in the attic?"

"Hey, I liked the attic. It was better than being at home." Then, as if he realized too late what he was saying, he seized the crate from her arms and walked out.

So maybe Kurt's life hadn't been so privileged after all. Well, that was certainly something to chew on some night when she couldn't sleep, Lissa thought.

She picked up another crate and followed him out to the Jaguar.

The steps were still piled with snow, but the front-room tenant was picking at the sidewalk with irregular thrusts of a ragged-edged snow shovel.

"Good exercise," Kurt commented as he walked past. "The repetitive arm motion builds the biceps—and that gets the girls' attention every time."

The tenant rolled his eyes. "So maybe *you* want to clear the sidewalk?"

"Oh, no," Kurt said pleasantly. "I already have my girl's attention, you see."

The tenant looked at Lissa as if he'd never seen her before. And perhaps, she thought, he hadn't—she'd certainly done her best to remain invisible around the boarding house. But suddenly a warm gleam of appreciation crept into his eyes.

She set the crate into the back of the Jaguar. "Gee, thanks," she said. "Now I suppose when I come home I'll have him on my doorstep asking for dates. You know, Kurt, if I wanted someone to advertise my good points I'd ask. But you wouldn't be the salesman I chose—so don't hold your breath."

He raised his eyebrows. "Advertising your good points? I was just trying to hurry him along to finish the sidewalk before one of us slips on the snow and falls down."

When they went back inside, the landlady was hovering suspiciously in the doorway of Lissa's room. "It sure looks like you're moving out," she accused. "The only things you've left are junk."

Lissa swallowed the retort she'd have liked to make—something about the landlady knowing junk when she saw it, since that was all the woman owned—and reached for another crate. This one was full of office supplies, and when she laid a board across the top, it served as her desk. She decided to leave the board behind. The landlady had finally moved on, and she decided to distract herself. "What is it with guys anyway?"

"Let's not start with the philosophical questions, Lissa."

"I'm serious. Why do men always seem more attracted to a woman after someone else has shown an interest in her? Even—" She bit her tongue. *Even in calculus class,* she'd started to say. The other young men had certainly looked at her with more interest after Kurt's tutoring session—at least in the few classes she'd managed to sit through before she'd cut and run.

"We want to make sure that other hunters agree that the quarry's worth going after, I suppose."

"Charming," Lissa muttered. "It's like being singled out as the meatiest mammoth in the herd."

Two trips later, the sidewalk was in much better condition. The shoveler paused to smile at her and lick his lips, and Lissa shuddered as she slid behind the wheel of Hannah's car.

Two weeks, she told herself. *I don't even have to think about it for two weeks.*

It was amazing how much stuff the woman thought she needed for a two-week stay, Kurt thought. Okay, he was responsible for her bringing the security blanket, but most of the rest had been her own idea. It had taken them far longer to load up all of Lissa's belongings than Kurt had expected it to, and when he carried in the first crate he was greeted with the scent of prime rib and fresh bread drifting through the house. At the top of the stairs, the guestroom sparkled, complete with robe and slippers laid out across the antique coverlet which covered the brass bed.

"There's no chocolate on the pillow," Lissa said. "And no fresh flowers."

He blinked in surprise. What an ungrateful little brat she was—to *complain!*

Then he saw the dazed look in her eyes as she looked around, and he took a minute to assess for himself the differences between Hannah's guestroom and the dark little hole they'd just left. Even at dusk on a winter afternoon the guestroom was bright and cheerful, airy and full of color and warmth, while he'd bet that at high noon on a sunny summer day the boarding house would look gloomy.

In fact, the only thing in the guestroom which wasn't particularly colorful was Lissa herself. She was still wearing the stark white tux shirt and black pants from her waitress shift earlier in the day, though she'd taken off the bow tie. And even her hair looked a little subdued—as if she were tired from head to foot.

I can work an hour here and there and fit partial shifts in between classes.

No wonder she was exhausted. But he thought it would be wiser not to share the suggestion which trembled on the tip of his tongue—that she might look better after a nap. Instead, he said mildly, "Well, the garden's covered with snow, and you had the car, so she couldn't go to the flower shop. I guess you'll have to do without the flowers."

"I just meant…." She shook her head. "I was being silly. This room is stunning. Those must be the drapes she thinks need to be replaced."

He could hear the incredulity in her voice, and he had to stop and think what she was talking about.

Oh, yes—Gran had said something about drapes in the midst of that litany of reasons why she wanted to sell the house. "I guess so. She did say guestroom, I think. But they look fine to me."

Lissa sighed. "Me, too. Better than fine, in fact."

"I'll go bring up another load." Kurt paused in the doorway. "You might want to change clothes before dinner. I caught a glimpse of silver in the dining room on my way up the stairs, so I think it's a dress-up occasion."

By the time he'd brought up the rest of her things Lissa had vanished into the bathroom. He stacked the last of the crates neatly along one wall of the guestroom, retreated to the attic bedroom to change his shirt, and went downstairs.

Janet and Gran had pulled out all the stops. The dining room table was laid with the heaviest and best of the silver flatware, and an old-fashioned epergne stood in the center, filled with oranges and apples and kiwi.

Hannah was sitting up very straight on a velvet chair in the living room, next to a flickering fire. She was wearing something lush and purple, with a row of sparkly clear stones around her neck.

She was staring out the front window, and for a moment Kurt thought she hadn't heard him come in. "Gran?"

"Oh, hello, dear. I assume you got all of Lissa's things moved?"

"Yes." The question left him feeling a bit uneasy. *All of Lissa's things*…. "Everything she could possibly need for a couple of weeks, anyway. You're not expecting her to stay longer than that—right?"

"How could she stay here, Kurt, if I'll be moving out myself?"

His grandmother's eyes were unusually bright, and Kurt wondered if she'd been sitting there staring into space, thinking about her move. Maybe even winking back a few tears. Lissa just might be right after all. If Gran was already having second thoughts….

Maybe we didn't need to pack up so much after all. A few days and Lissa might be headed straight back home…in a manner of speaking. Well, when it came time to shift it all back, he'd gladly pay a mover.

"Can I get you a sherry?" he asked.

His grandmother smiled. "That would be lovely, dear."

He was standing at the sideboard in the dining room when he heard the creak of a stair. Third one from the bottom—he remembered it well from trying to sneak in after his curfew, before he'd learned how to climb the oak tree and swing over the rail of the attic balcony to let himself in.

He poured a second sherry. It probably wasn't the drink Lissa would choose—he suspected she'd rather have a beer—but if she was going to live under his grandmother's roof for a couple of weeks she'd better at least be introduced to the sherry ritual.

He turned toward the living room, saw her standing at the foot of the stairs with one hand still on the newel post, and stopped dead.

There was nothing outstanding about the dress Lissa wore—neither the cut nor the fabric shouted for attention, and he'd bet it had come from an anonymous designer and a discount rack. But the deep rich color fell somewhere between ordinary blue and ordinary green, and ended up not being ordinary at all. She didn't look like a faded photo anymore—she was once more vivid and brilliant and stunning.

And the cut—commonplace though it would probably look on another woman—was anything but common on Lissa. There was still no doubt in his mind that she was too slender. But when she was clad in something more feminine than the tux shirt and black pants she wasn't at all the stick he'd expected. The way the dress draped around her body drew his gaze upward to a slim, straight neck, and downward to slim, straight legs. And then he lingered over a whole lot of soft and gentle curves in between.

Soft and gentle curves she hadn't had six years ago. He'd have remembered those, just as clearly as he remembered the way she'd slowly come to life as he'd kissed her…the way she'd sparkled as he made love to her…the way she'd made him catch fire….

You wouldn't have heard a brass band that night either, Callahan.

He must have made some kind of a sound, for his grandmother looked over her shoulder at him. "My goodness, dear, I thought for a moment you were choking."

No, Gran, only acting like those guys at the cloakroom counter last night. He handed his grandmother a glass, holding another out to Lissa. "Would you like sherry, Lissa?"

"Yes, please." Her fingers brushed his as she took the crystal glass, half full of amber liquid, and Kurt felt something shift deep inside him, like the first warning tremor of an earthquake. She wasn't even smiling at him, but the lights in the room seemed to dim in comparison.

The woman was dangerous, he told himself. She always had been—even more so when she looked the most innocent. And, if he was smart, he wouldn't let himself forget it.

Maximum Sports' newest and biggest store had already been open for business for several weeks, in order to take advantage of the enormous potential offered by holiday gift-buying. But the formal grand opening celebration had been put off till this week—both for the sake of making a bigger splash and so Kurt could be present.

There were thirty-seven stores, and he hadn't missed a grand opening yet—though now that they were considering selling franchises it might not be quite so easy to keep up the pace. Still, even after thirty-seven times, Kurt enjoyed the thrill of cutting the ribbon to formally unveil a new location. This was the fun part of his job—talking to employees who were excited about the new store, listening to customers as they exclaimed over the variety and style of the merchandise, and watching as golf clubs and snowboards and bicycles surged through the checkout lines.

And, of course, he enjoyed personally demonstrating a few of the things that made Maximum Sports so different from other sports outfitters.

In his position halfway up the climbing wall, he braced himself for a brief rest and looked down at the crowd watching his progress. The wall was sixty feet tall, and though climbing it wasn't exactly a challenge on the same level as Mount Everest, it was no walk on the beach. He was at the point now where the wall began to curve back over his head, making the rest of the climb similar to dangling over thin air while scrambling up an overhanging knob of rock.

Nobody to blame but yourself, Callahan, he thought. The climbing walls in most of the stores had been built with beginners in mind, and even this one had a couple of easier sections. But he'd designed this bit himself, based on a particularly challenging outcrop on a mountain he'd climbed in Peru last year. It should be a piece of cake after defeating the original.

He looked out over the crowd. Mostly young women, he saw. *What a surprise.*

A flash of red hair caught his eye, but it wasn't Lissa. There was no tiny gray-haired lady beside her. Where were they, anyway? Cracked up somewhere on the freeway? He should have known better than to rely on her driving skills….

His toe slipped from the foothold and the crowd gasped. Half were frightened, Kurt thought, and half were anticipating the possibility that the head of Maximum Sports might end up splattered at the bottom of the climbing wall. Which was why they had the rule that no one could be on the wall without a safety harness and a trained belaying partner.

He got his breath back and moved on before the crowd could lose interest and wander off.

He didn't see Gran and Lissa come in, but twenty minutes later, when he reached the floor once more, his grandmother was chatting to the weight-lifter lookalike who was paying out Kurt's safety ropes. "We simply couldn't keep him on the ground as a youngster," she was saying. "He climbed out of his crib before he was ten months old, and he climbed up the bookshelves in the library when he was two. And then there was the time he tried to fly off the garage roof with a kite in each hand…."

"Learned my lesson on that one," Kurt said.

"What? How to build a bigger kite?" Lissa murmured.

He shed the harness—not his favorite piece of equipment, since it tended to be warmer than was comfortable. "You finally got here, I see. You missed the best part."

She was still looking up at the wall. Her hands were buried in the pockets of her coat—the same oversized, old-fashioned man's wool tweed overcoat she'd been wearing yesterday. On her slender frame it managed to look like a fashion statement rather than a castoff.

Kurt mopped his forehead with a towel. "How much of the demonstration did you watch?"

"Enough," Lissa said. He looked more closely; she seemed to be a little pale around the edges. "That's what you do for fun?"

"I'd rather do it on real mountains, without all the safety ropes. But, since Minneapolis is smack in the middle of the flatlands, I take what I can get. I suppose your reaction means you don't want to give the wall a try?"

"You got that much right. I'll stick to writing tax software, thanks."

"Just as well—because all of today's slots are already reserved anyway. Where have you been, Gran? I thought you were coming over first thing this morning."

"We were busy with the Christmas tree."

Kurt frowned. "I expected you'd wait for me to help put it up."

"You sound like a disappointed six-year-old. Anyway, it's not up yet," his grandmother said. "We were just trying to find one."

"What's wrong with the tree you always use?"

"I decided to have a real one. I've always wanted a live tree, but Janet thinks they're a fire hazard. This year I decided to set my foot down and buy one anyway—but you have no idea how hard it is to find a nice-sized tree."

"That's too bad," he said. "Of course, it *is* getting pretty late in the season."

"So when will you be home? We need a man to get it balanced properly."

"I thought you said you couldn't find one."

"It just took longer than I expected. I think we've looked at every tree for sale on this side of the city," his grandmother said proudly. "I was just about to suggest that we go out in the country and find a tree farm, but we finally found what I wanted. It'll take all of us to get it wrestled into place, I think."

He shot a glance at Lissa, who seemed to be studying a display of ropes and crampons. She looked guilty—there was no other word for it. "How big is this tree, exactly?"

"I figure we'll need to use every ornament in the house if we decorate it properly," his grandmother said. "Which is lovely, because then when the tree comes down after the holidays I can sort all the decorations out and set aside a boxful for each member of the family—the special things that will have memories for them. There are at least a dozen ornaments somewhere that you made in grade school. You used to send me one for Christmas each year. Remember?"

"I've done my best to forget. How did you get this thing home? Tie it on top of the car? That must have been a sight."

Lissa shifted her feet. "Well, that's something we should probably talk about."

He groaned. "I suppose you want me to take charge? All right—tell me where it is."

She looked doubtful. "Are you offering to pick it up in the Jaguar?"

"Of course not. The store has delivery trucks."

Lissa looked around. "At the rate people are buying treadmills and weight benches, we might get a delivery by New Year's Day."

"I'm the boss. They'll do what I tell them."

"And you're so good at bossing, too," his grandmother said warmly. "At any rate, don't concern yourself about the tree—we've got that all figured out. Now, let's get out of the way and let him go back to being the boss, Lissa."

"I'll walk you out," he said. "I could use a little fresh air after that climb, anyway."

The crowd made navigating difficult. Hannah dawdled behind for a while, looking at sports socks on an end cap, and then, making up her mind, hurried ahead of them toward the checkout lanes with some merchandise in hand.

Kurt felt like the first skier on a run after a big snow—it was exhausting just to break a trail through the crowd.

They reached the entrance, and Kurt leaned against one of the granite pillars just inside the main doors. A woman—not much more than a teenager—who was just coming in from the parking lot spotted him, flicked a hand over her hair, batted her eyes, and shifted course to come straight toward him.

"They start young, don't they?" Lissa murmured. She leaned against the pillar next to him and eyed the young woman, and to Kurt's utter amazement the woman flushed pink and veered off toward camping goods.

"How did you do that?" he asked.

"Do what? All I did was look at her. I think she just got cold feet when you glared. About this Christmas tree, Kurt." She sighed. "I think Hannah saw my little tree yesterday when you carried it in. It was right on top of a crate, and I think that's what gave her the notion."

"Oh—of course." He remembered his own reaction to seeing that pathetic, straggly little artificial tree with its five too-big ornaments. Gran, sentimental old darling that she was, would have felt even more strongly that anyone who could cherish such a bedraggled little tree deserved a real one.

"So if you want to blame me," Lissa said, "I guess you can go right ahead."

"Oh, what the hell?" he said. "It's her last Christmas in the house—she should have whatever she wants."

His grandmother came up to them, triumphantly waving a shopping bag emblazoned with the penguin which was Maximum Sports' mascot and logo, and he pushed the door open for her.

Lissa shot a look up at him. "I'm really glad you feel that way," she murmured.

Kurt's veins prickled—and not just because of the cold wind. There was something about her tone...

He scanned the parking lot, looking for the small, faded red car, and blinked in astonishment as his grandmother stopped beside a very different vehicle. A dark green and obviously spanking new sport utility vehicle. And on top of it, neatly bound with rope and tied down tight with bungee cords—

It wasn't the tallest pine tree he'd ever seen, but it was certainly the longest he'd ever encountered in a horizontal position. At least he thought it was—but his eyes seemed to be freezing solid in the brisk wind so he wasn't quite certain what he was looking at. "Gran, what's this?"

She smiled merrily. "Isn't it nice? They call it a sieve, or something like that, I can't think why. Have you got the keys, Lissa? I'll put this stuff in the back."

"An SUV," he said faintly. "You bought an SUV just so you could get your tree home, Gran?"

"Of course not," she said indignantly.

Kurt gave a small sigh of relief. That sounded more like his grandmother. Renting the vehicle for the day, or borrowing it from a good-hearted neighbor, would make a great deal more sense than actually buying it.

"We'll be hauling all kinds of stuff as we clear the house out," his grandmother said, "and it would have been simply too hard for Lissa to get big boxes of things in and out of that little car. So I decided to make it easier on her."

His jaw had dropped, and now his tongue was starting to freeze.

"Besides," his grandmother went on, "the nice salesman gave me a whole lot more money for my car than you thought it was worth, so trading ended up being much more sensible than just selling it for taxi fare. And you did tell Lissa to buy me new tires, so—"

Kurt sputtered, "Dammit, Lissa, you told her about the tires?"

She sounded defensive. "Well, you didn't actually say I shouldn't mention it. And I thought if she understood that you really would like to do something for her—"

Kurt couldn't even find his voice.

Hannah said, "You thought I'd turn down the gift

if I knew about it, didn't you? But Lissa was very convincing that I should let you make things easier for me." Hannah opened the passenger door and stood back to show it off. "Isn't this nice? See how the little board slides out automatically, so I have a step? Don't forget to give him the bill, Lissa." She climbed up into the SUV and firmly closed the door.

"The bill? You mean the bill for the—?"

Lissa was very convincing that I should let you make things easier for me.

Lisa looked at him with a gleam in her eyes that made him long to choke her. Then she pulled a sheaf of paper out of the pocket of her overcoat.

Kurt muttered, "Gran *would* be the one person on the planet to get confused about the difference between *a set of tires* and *a set of wheels*. I didn't intend to buy her a whole—"

"Remember?" Lissa chided. "You said you're not the one who has the cheap streak. Well, here's your chance to prove it. And from now on when you ride with me you won't feel you're in a tomato soup can!"

CHAPTER FOUR

IT HAD TAKEN Lissa most of the afternoon to feel truly warm again after being out in the brisk wind so much of the morning. Shopping for a Christmas tree, wandering through the dealer's entire assortment of SUVs, and then standing in the parking lot discussing both purchases with Kurt had left her chilled to the bone.

So she wasn't at all surprised when Kurt came into the living room late in the afternoon and without a word went straight to the fireplace to hold his hands over the flames. He'd been out in that parking lot without even a coat when he'd still been perspiring from his stunt on the climbing wall. It would be no wonder if he was feeling the after-effects of that knife-edged wind even hours later.

The room felt different to Lissa the moment he walked in—though it wasn't so much the gust of cold air he brought with him as something far less tangible. The tang of testosterone, she told herself wryly, watching him out of the corner of her eye from her cross-legged position on the carpet almost under the Christmas tree. The air seemed to sparkle with the power of his presence.

He'd changed out of the stretchy, close-fitting climbing gear he'd been wearing in the store that morning and into a bulky sweater and wool trousers. She preferred him in street clothes, she decided, because the hardness and strength of his body weren't quite so blatant. That didn't mean he was easy to ignore, of course—the man still moved like a well-oiled machine. But at least every muscle wasn't obvious, as it had been this morning, reminding her with his every twitch that once—just once, so long ago—she had stroked those muscles and luxuriated in the warmth and power of his body....

It was a one-night stand, she reminded herself rudely. *A bad soap opera, not classic literature. Get over it.*

"Have a cup of tea," she suggested. "It's a fresh pot."

Kurt turned his back to the fire, as if to baste his spine in warmth. "I'd rather have a stiff Scotch."

Lissa shook her head. "Alcohol doesn't warm you up, it only fools you into thinking you're comfortable." She reached for another box—this one simply marked *Xmas decorations*—and wondered what was likely to be in it. She'd already unearthed a *papier-maché* nativity set, a collection of angels which took her breath away, and an assortment of Santa statues which could outfit a gift shop at the North Pole.

"I'm more interested in its pain-killing properties. The fire's taking the edge off the cold, but it would help my attitude immensely if you weren't playing 'Let It Snow' in the background."

Lissa considered turning up the volume. Instead, she got up and poured him a cup from the still-steaming teapot. "Here. At least drink this first. It'll warm you up *and* improve your mood. If anything can."

"Watch out, Lissa. Someone might think you're concerned about me."

She sank down beside the stack of boxes once more. "I've had pneumonia, and I wouldn't wish it on my worst enemy. Of course, you *deserve* to get at least a good old-fashioned cold. Standing in the parking lot in your shirtsleeves like that, even if you hadn't still been soaked from doing your stunt on that wall thing—"

"That *wall thing* is one of the most popular features of my stores."

"Popular, maybe. Profitable, no way. It can't possibly be, after you pay the insurance costs."

"I have a perfectly good team of accountants, Lissa, so anytime you're finished imitating a professional you can stop analyzing my business."

She felt herself color with irritation. All right, maybe she had been showing off a bit, making it clear that she knew a few things about profits and losses—but did he have to clip her quite so hard just because she didn't have a set of letters after her name yet?

"The wall draws people in to watch or to climb," he pointed out. "And once they're in the store, they usually buy something."

"Of course I know profit isn't the only motive for offering a service. But—never mind." She shifted a particularly heavy box, deliberately turning her back to him.

"I see you got the tree set up without my help."

Lissa didn't even look over her shoulder at him. "The handyman was here to finish clearing the snow off the walks, so your grandmother enlisted him." She took a deep breath of pine scent. The tree's fragrance was gradually filling the room as the branches relaxed in the warmth.

"This was the biggest one the two of you could find, right?"

"It's a little larger than I thought it was," Lissa admitted. The spread of the tree's lowest limbs took up almost half the width of the room.

Kurt drained the teacup and went to pour himself a drink from the cabinet in the dining room. "Want a glass of wine or something?"

Lissa shook her head. "Sorting out these boxes is making me dizzy enough, thanks."

"Where's Gran, by the way? I thought decorating this tree was her pet project."

"Well, she's pretty good at delegating the parts she doesn't want to do. I don't suppose *you'd* want to work on untangling the strings of lights?"

"Good guess."

"Hannah would like the lights to be on so she can start decorating after her nap."

"Then you have your job cut out for you. She's taking another nap?"

"What's wrong with a nap every afternoon? She's had a busy day. When we were looking for just the right tree she was inexhaustible—but an eighty-year-old woman can't keep up that pace forever."

"And then there was the SUV to buy," Kurt said. "Why did you let her do that, anyway?"

"*Let* her?" Lissa's voice was an incredulous squeak. "I'd have liked to see *you* stop her, once she got the notion in her head!"

He went straight on without apology. "That's the big question, you know. Just how *did* she get the notion in her head?"

"All I told her was that you wanted her to have new, safe tires, and you'd make it part of her Christmas gift. In fact, I asked her if she wanted me to take care of it so she wouldn't have to bother. She said no, she'd talk to her favorite mechanic to get some advice about what sort of tires would be best for her car. Of course as soon as she set foot in the dealership—"

"The salespeople were on her like vultures, I suppose."

"They didn't exactly take advantage of her," Lissa said reluctantly. "All the salespeople were busy, in fact—so she wandered around, looking at all the tires in the showroom. Then her feet started to hurt and she decided to sit down inside an SUV, and when she spotted the friendly little running board sliding out to help her climb in she fell in love."

Kurt groaned.

"Then it was just a question of which color she wanted. We had to look at every one they had in stock so she could decide. I didn't realize there were so many colors. If you're worried about the money—"

"I'm not." His voice was clipped.

"Well, I wouldn't blame you if you were," she said with mock sympathy. "It can't be cheap to start up yet another brand-new store, and when you've got a whole chain in expansion mode—"

"I'm not in any financial difficulty, but thanks for your concern."

"I'm very glad to hear it. Anyway, what I was just going to tell you is that Hannah was only joking about you paying for her new car."

"And I suppose that's why you handed me the bill?"

"Obviously you still haven't looked at those papers. If you had just listened to me this morning instead of shoving everything in your pocket and walking away—"

"Are you nuts? If I hadn't walked away I'd still

be standing there. Only by now I'd be imitating an ice sculpture."

"It would be the perfect job for you," Lissa muttered. "If you'd stuck around for thirty seconds longer I would have told you that she wrote a check for it."

Kurt's eyebrows had raised a fraction. "She paid the entire amount?"

"All except the tires. She seemed to think that was a really good joke." She lifted the lid off the heavy box and peered inside. "You wouldn't happen to know why Hannah would have spray-painted a bunch of bricks bright red and packed them up with the Christmas stuff, would you?"

Kurt shrugged. "Not a clue."

Lissa stacked the bricks neatly to one side, set the box into the pile of empties, and dragged the next carton over in front of her. "And that's another subject, you know. Keeping that sort of money lying around in an ordinary demand deposit account makes no sense whatsoever when she could be earning interest on it."

"Oh, I don't know. A checking account seems a whole lot smarter to me than keeping cash in an envelope in a boarding house."

"I'll do my best to remember that next time I have a small fortune to invest. My point is, she could be earning a lot more in a money market fund than in an ordinary checking account."

"Now that it's spent," Kurt said, "it doesn't seem to matter much where she had it stashed. In an envelope, under her mattress, at the bank—what's the difference? What's she going to do with a vehicle like that in a retirement village?"

"Take all her friends out for joyrides, I suppose."

"Who's going to drive? Are you planning to extend your two weeks into permanent employment?"

Lissa felt a little stab of regret. Two weeks—and one of her precious fourteen days of freedom was already nearly gone. "Of course not. By then she'll have seen a doctor, and maybe with an adjustment in her medication she'll be able to drive again."

"Oh, that would be a real relief," he said dryly. "Gran at the controls of a sport utility vehicle—"

"Well, you have to admit she'll be safer in the SUV than in the tomato can, no matter who's behind the wheel."

"That's true," he conceded. "I'm not convinced there's a penny's worth of difference between the two of you when it comes to driving skills."

She shot a narrow look at him over the box she'd just opened, which seemed to be full of garishly colored needlepoint Christmas stockings.

"Retirement villages provide transportation," Kurt said. "Buses and vans and wheelchair lifts and all that stuff. The residents don't have to drive at all."

"Maybe, but I can't quite see Hannah scheduling her massage times to fit the bus driver's schedule.

Maybe she really bought the SUV because she's planning to have you take her mountain climbing? There's plenty of room for the gear in the back, plus four-wheel drive so you can go off-road and rough it."

"Gran? Don't be ridiculous."

Lissa shook out a ruffled lace tree skirt which had been crushed under the needlepoint stockings and pretended not to look at him. "You didn't seem to want her to move into a retirement village anyway. What's your plan? That she move in with you instead?"

She was a little surprised that he didn't react to the bait. Instead he planted one hip against the arm of the couch, right above where she was working, and meditatively swirled his drink.

"You're looking a little flushed," she said. "Are you feeling all right? Because pneumonia can really—"

"You can stop trying so hard to convince me you had pneumonia, Lissa."

She was startled. "What? Why would I lie to you about—?"

"I'm convinced. Your background check said it was quite a case you had."

She gritted her teeth. "You ran a background check on me?"

"Sure." His tone was casual. "I do it with all employees—of course I'd want to know that my grandmother's personal assistant wasn't a felon on the run. Why does it bother you so much that I looked into your past, anyway?"

She swallowed hard. "It doesn't bother me, exactly. It just took me by surprise."

"Sure it did. You know, Lissa, it makes me wonder—if there *is* something you want to hide, what might it be? You were so eager to tell me why you had to drop out—your father being ill, your pneumonia. I couldn't help but wonder if the real story was just a little more."

"Like that wouldn't be enough," Lissa muttered. "So what were you expecting to find?"

He rattled the ice in his glass and said, very clearly, "A baby."

The silver glass ball she'd just picked up slipped from her hand and shattered on the floor. *What on earth had given him that idea?* "You mean... like...*your* baby?"

"The possibility occurred to me. The way you disappeared from that calculus class...and talk I heard from people who'd seen you around the university —"

"Your pals from class were spying on me, I suppose?"

"It's not a huge campus, Lissa. But they just thought you looked miserable. It didn't occur to me that you might actually have been ill. Or pregnant. Anyway, I'd forgotten all about that till—"

"Fine time to be thinking about it now. This baby you're postulating would be five years old," she said.

"Yes, and I feel bad about that. But I didn't know

that you'd dropped out of school. I had no reason to be suspicious back then."

"So why now?"

He hesitated. "Yesterday, when you started talking about how in some situations there aren't any good choices, I started to wonder exactly what you meant."

"And because of that you thought I was telling you I'd had your baby?" Her voice was tart. "And what did you think I'd done with this supposed infant?"

"Given it up for adoption, I suppose."

"And what would you have done about it now?"

He looked down into his glass. "I don't know."

Lissa's heart twisted just a little. "Well, I hope you're satisfied that it never happened."

"You had a father with lymphoma, followed by a bad case of pneumonia."

Lissa shrugged. "Exactly what I told you."

The doorbell chimed, and Lissa pushed a box aside and got to her feet, groaning a little as her knees protested at the length of time she'd been on the floor.

As she pulled the door open, the bells on the wreath she had hung there jingled gaily.

Hannah's friend Marian was standing on the wide front porch, her fingertip already pushing the bell a second time. "Sorry," Marian said, not sounding as if she meant it. "Janet's getting hard of hearing, you know. What on earth are *you* doing here? I barely recognized you out of uniform." Her gaze drifted over Lissa's jeans and sweater.

"I'm helping out a bit, Mrs. Meadows," Lissa said coolly.

"Oh, yes, of course. I heard Hannah had a fainting spell after I left the restaurant the other day, so I came to check on her." Marian brushed past Lissa, already taking off her hat. "Goodness, it's cold out there."

Lissa took the hint and stepped back politely. "Would you like a cup of tea? Mrs. Wilder is having a nap, but I expect she'll be downstairs soon. Kurt's here."

Marian looked past her, as if to check out what Lissa had said, just as Kurt appeared in the pillared archway between the living room and the foyer. "In that case I'll come in. It's too bad that my little friend couldn't come along today. I guess you'll have to wait for that treat, Kurt."

She sounded, Lissa thought, as if she was denying a five-year-old a ride on a carousel. *Little friend?* How corny could the woman get, anyway?

Marian bustled past Kurt into the living room and stopped dead. "What is going on in here?"

"Just some holiday decorating," Lissa said. "I hope you won't mind if I keep right on working after I pour your tea."

"Not at all." Marian didn't even look at her. "In fact, I'll pour, and Kurt and I will just sit down here at the other end of the room, where we'll be out of your way."

"Sorry, Marian," Kurt said smoothly, "but I'm helping Lissa untangle the lights. Since she was good enough to volunteer to help decorate, I couldn't possibly leave her to face the consequences if it isn't all done by the time Gran wakes up."

Not that it was exactly a compliment, Lissa thought, to know that he'd rather be on her end of the room unpacking boxes than drinking tea with Marian….

The man had seriously entertained the notion that she'd had his baby? After six long years, what had made him contemplate the possibility now?

"But help yourself to tea," he went on cheerfully. His voice dropped to a murmur that tickled Lissa's ear. "Quick—where are the lights?"

I should ignore him. But Lissa used her foot to push a box toward him. "As long as we're talking about weird hypotheses…do you also believe the moon landing was a fake?"

"I had reason to be suspicious, Lissa."

"Because I told you I'd dropped out for a while? Honestly…." She took a deep breath and decided it would be prudent to change the subject. "Never mind. I had no idea you were such a coward, by the way."

"Coward? Me?"

"Yes—running from a simple thing like Marian's 'little friend.' And she isn't even here to run from— that's what's so hilarious."

"Better to squelch the whole idea up front. The

only thing worse than an elderly matchmaker is a pair of them."

"I suppose that's true. Is this the little friend you had mixed up with me?"

Kurt lifted the lid of the box and heaved a huge sigh. "Next time look for an electrical engineer to do this job." He dug both hands into the box and pulled out a gnarled mass of dark green wires and small multicolored bulbs. "And if you're expecting me to admit that I'd rather Marian's friend *had* been you—"

"Heavens, no. I wouldn't want you to break your long-standing record and actually be flattering to me."

Marian was coming back toward them, cup in hand. "I had no idea you knew Hannah so well that you'd volunteer to give up your Christmas break to help her." Her voice took on a cool edge. "Or is this a chance to earn some extra money?"

"Actually," Lissa said sweetly, "I haven't been acquainted with Hannah all that long. It's Kurt I've known forever, so of course I'm happy to lend a hand wherever I can to help his grandmother."

"I'm quite sure of *that*." Marian's voice had gone icy.

From the foot of the stairs, Hannah said, "Marian, how delightful of you to drop by! Rae didn't come with you?"

"No, darling, because I didn't expect Kurt to be here this afternoon. But we could stop by tomorrow, if the two of you will be free."

"Don't count on it," Kurt said under his breath. "There must be twenty strands of lights in here." He found a plug and untangled enough cord to reach the outlet. Just three of the tiny bulbs lit up. "We've known each other forever, hmm? I think all those Christmas carols are starting to rot your brain."

"Hey, I'm not the one who's into conspiracy theories." Lissa turned back to the box she'd just opened, which seemed to contain nothing but crocheted snowflakes. The starch which stiffened them had yellowed with age. "And even you have to admit it does feel like forever. Besides, it would be foolish for me to pretend I've been Hannah's friend when all Marian would have to do is ask and she'd find out differently."

The bigger question, Lissa asked herself, was why she'd said anything at all. So what if Marian Meadows took a swipe at her? Why on earth had she implied that she and Kurt were pals, and had been forever?

They'd never been friends, though once—for a painfully brief span of time—she'd thought they might be more than friends. Much more. But that had been only an illusion, and he'd stripped it from her as quickly and painfully as an adhesive bandage peeled off skin. So what had inspired her to say it now?

Janet had appeared with a fresh pot of tea and a plate of cookies still warm from the oven. She set them on the coffee table at the far end of the room, and the two women settled down on the couch there. Though Lissa wasn't trying to overhear their conversation, Marian's slightly shrill voice made it impossible to ignore her.

"I hope your new helper is working out well," Marian said. "I wouldn't have thought of hiring her, myself. But it makes perfect sense. As a waitress, she's used to this sort of work—fetching and carrying and general picking up. Though it must be very uncomfortable for her, having to be a hanger-on at someone else's holidays."

Kurt seemed to be talking to the box of tangled wires. "I bet the woman's a lousy tipper."

"Not *lousy*, exactly," Lissa felt compelled to say. "She's very correct and proper. Fifteen percent, right down to the penny."

"Charming. Just the sort of woman I want to know better—and her *little friend*, too. I've got it. Let's drag out the decorating till tomorrow, and when she and the pal show up for tea we can be gone buying new lights."

She must have looked at him oddly, because he went on, "I'm not talking about some sort of date, you know. It's only to buy lights."

"Oh, I'm glad you clarified that. Thanks for the invitation, but I'm simply dying to meet Rae."

"If I felt safe leaving you here to talk to Rae, I'd go get the lights by myself."

Lissa set a stack of snowflakes aside. "Besides,

Hannah would never approve. Wasting money on lights that will only be used once? How foolish."

"I'm paying—it'll be worth it to be able to throw these away. After Christmas she can hang them all over her SUV if she wants." He raised his voice. "Gran, you don't mind if I buy all new lights for the tree, do you? Untangling these is a waste of time, and you don't have enough anyway."

"You can do whatever you want, dear. But you'll need to get them tonight, so we can have the tree nice and neat for tomorrow when Marian's bringing Rae. So run along, both of you, and take care of it right now." Hannah smiled. "You can take my new sieve if you like."

The look of chagrin on Kurt's face made it difficult for Lissa to smother a laugh. "Next time," she managed to say, "you might try selling her on tinsel instead of lights. That goes on *after* everything else."

It didn't take Lissa choking on her own amusement to let Kurt know he'd been had once more—and it was no consolation at all to know that this time he'd pretty much done it to himself.

"All right," Kurt said. "Let's go." He dragged Lissa's coat out of the closet and warily eyed the keyring she pulled out of her pocket. "I'm sure not riding with you. We're taking my car."

"That's fine with me. This is your errand anyway—I was only hired to do your grandmother's running around. In fact, there's no reason for me to go at all." She started to slide out of her coat.

Kurt grabbed her arm. "I want to talk to you. But not where the pacemaker generation can overhear."

"What about? If you're still going on about this baby—"

"No."

"You believe me?" She wanted to put an end to it.

"Let's say I believe in the background check."

"Oh, that's a comfort." She subsided, and let him usher her out the side door. "So what's this about, really?"

"Lights."

"Honest? Well, you should have seen that one coming a mile away. Now what are you going to use for an excuse to be gone at teatime tomorrow?"

"I'll think of something." The Jaguar skidded sideways as he pulled out into the street just a little too fast for the road conditions.

"You're sure you don't want to take the SUV? You'd have better traction on slick streets with those new tires."

Kurt shot a look at her.

Lissa bit her lip as if to hold back a smile, and sank into the smooth leather seat of the Jaguar. "I was only trying to be helpful," she murmured. "So what did you want to talk to me about?"

"The lights were a bad idea."

"No kidding."

"If I avoid Marian's little friend tomorrow, they'll just set up another time."

"Not that you have an inflated opinion of how far someone will go to meet you, of course. Sorry—I didn't mean to interrupt. You're probably right. Marian doesn't seem the sort to give up easily."

"If I'm not there at teatime, they'll stay for dinner."

"And if you miss dinner…." She sounded almost thoughtful, except for the tang of laughter in her voice. "You know, it might be interesting to see if they'd actually turn up for breakfast."

What was it going to take for her to treat this seriously? "I have a better idea. I'm going to meet What's-her-name—"

"Rae."

"As scheduled tomorrow. Only *you're* going to be with me."

She sounded wary. "With you…how?"

"I'll be polite and civil and obviously not intrigued by Rae because I'm interested in someone else. You, to be precise. You've already laid the groundwork by telling Marian we've known each other forever. So when she and the pal show up tomorrow we'll go into our more-than-friends act—"

"Wait a minute. *More than* friends? I didn't even say we were friends, much less—"

"That's the beauty of it. She'll be up all night, working out the possible interpretations, and by tomorrow she'll be easy to convince that her little pal doesn't stand a chance with me as long as you're around."

"And you think *my* brain's rotting?" Lissa shook her head. "I can't imagine why you think that would work."

"I got the idea at the store this morning, when you ran off that woman at the door."

Lissa stared. "I did what?"

"You took one look at her and she veered off course like a bad torpedo."

"But not because of anything *I* did. There's nothing to say she ever really intended to come over to you."

"She did. I know."

She looked at him thoughtfully. "How many warehouses does it take just to store your ego, Kurt?"

"The point is, I don't know how you waved her off, and I don't care. Just as long as you do it again tomorrow."

"By scaring Rae into a retreat? Honestly, Kurt, why you suddenly think you need a bodyguard to protect you from Rae—"

"If you want to know what's in it for you, Lissa…."

"Oh, yes, please—tell me what the reward is here." Lissa tossed her head back against the seat, and soft-looking hair met soft leather. The static electricity made a few of the auburn strands stand up straight. His fingertips itched to smooth them back in place.

Almost too late he realized what he was thinking and drew his hand back to a safe distance.

Watch it, Callahan. It's a good idea you've got—as long as you remember that she's dangerous. It's not smart to play with dynamite, but if you use it carefully....

"You're hoping your grandmother gets annoyed and fires me, aren't you? Well, I'm not playing along. Because I have a better plan."

"I'm listening."

"Actually, it's your plan—just without me. All you have to do is be cool and polite to Rae tomorrow and see what happens. It's one day, Kurt. What's the big deal?"

"What about the rest of the week?" He pulled up at a traffic light and looked over at her, taking just a bit of malicious pleasure in the dismay which gleamed in her eyes.

"The rest of the week?" she said lamely. "You told me your grand opening would be over on Sunday."

"And it will. But surely..." The light changed and he eased the Jaguar into the intersection. "Surely you didn't expect me to go home and leave my grandmother to celebrate Christmas all by herself. Did you?"

They bought all the lights they could find in two different stores, but they were still arguing about Marian's friend and what to do about her when they returned to the house. Lissa was chilled by the weather but heated by the discussion. She was so absorbed that she didn't even see the extra car parked under the porte cochere until Kurt stopped the Jaguar just short of the bumper.

"Where did that come from?" she asked.

"Considering the emblem on the front, I'd say Japan," Kurt said dryly. "It's not Marian's, because it wasn't there when we left."

"No doubt Rae's lying in wait for you, right inside the door."

"I wouldn't put it past Marian. What about it, Lissa?"

"You mean The Great Friendship Escapade? You've never been particularly good at being straightforward with women, have you? Maybe it's time you had some practice."

"What in the hell does that mean? If you'd have just listened to me back then—"

"To what? You justifying how you hadn't *really* made a bet with your friends that you could get me to go to bed with you?"

"I didn't."

"Oh, please—let's not start arguing over definitions. It's over. Your friends took care of letting me know where I stood, so you didn't have to. And that's exactly what you're trying to do again. Only instead of me being the dupe this time, you want me to run interference for you. Well, I'm not interested.

Deal with Rae yourself." She dug a pile of boxes from the back seat. The wrappings were slick, and the boxes seemed to want to slide off to every point of the compass.

Kurt had an equally large and awkward stack, but he managed to get them tucked under his arm so he could open the side door of the house. Rather than put the boxes down to take off her coat, Lissa went straight to the living room to dump the new lights under the tree.

Kurt was barely a step behind her when she crossed the threshold and saw the new addition to the tea party. Only now it was more of a cocktail party, she realized, with crystal glasses and clinking ice rather than teacups, and three people forming an uneven triangle—Hannah and Marian on the couch, and standing nearby, one hand braced on the mantel….

Lissa blinked in surprise. Then she realized what had happened—what must have happened—and tried to push down the bubble of laughter which was threatening to explode deep inside her.

"There you are, Kurt," Marian said. "I've been so eager for you to meet my young friend that I decided not to wait till tomorrow in case you couldn't be here after all." She pointed at the young man standing by the mantel. "This," Marian went on proudly, "is Ray."

CHAPTER FIVE

LISSA BIT HER tongue as hard as she could, trying to turn her gasp of amusement into a cough or a gulp. But nothing could stop the delight she'd felt when she saw the look on Kurt's face as he caught sight of Ray.

It was all she could do to get herself out of the room before she lost control completely. "I must go take my coat off," she managed to babble. "It's awfully warm in here." She bent to set down the lights under the tree, but the boxes slipped and sprayed out of her hands. Lissa didn't stop to pick them up; as it was, she barely made it to the foyer before she doubled over, clutching her tummy and trying to hold back a shriek of laughter.

Kurt had made such a mighty effort to avoid being matched up with Marian's little friend—and then Ray turned out to be a *guy*. No wonder Marian had made it sound as if she was promising a little boy a playmate!

Lissa held onto the newel post and tried not to howl—there was, after all, only a pillar, a thin wall, and the crackle of the fire to block any sound she made from the guests' ears.

Kurt was only a few steps behind her. "What in the—?"

"If you could see yourself," Lissa gasped. She slid out of her overcoat and draped it over the bannister.

"Would you stop?" Kurt said. "This isn't funny."

"Well, it might not be from your perspective, but it's pretty hilarious from where I'm sitting." She suited the action to the words, sinking down on the lowest step. "All the effort you went to, trying to manipulate me into helping you, and not a bit of it was necessary!" She tried to gulp back another laugh, but the effort went wrong and she began to cough instead.

Kurt dropped down beside her and slapped her lightly between the shoulders.

Lissa pulled away. "Hey, you don't have to beat on me."

"I'm just trying to keep you from choking to death now so I can have the joy of strangling you with my own hands later." But he stopped patting her back.

"You can't possibly blame *me* for this," Lissa argued. "I'm not the one with such a tremendous ego that I jumped to conclusions. You really should get over yourself, Kurt. The very idea that women are standing in line to be noticed, scheming to be introduced—"

Kurt heaved a sigh and leaned back, elbows propped on a stair. "Enjoy yourself."

"Oh, I will. It never even occurred to you that Ray might be a guy, did it?"

"I don't recall you expressing doubts on the subject, either."

"The look on your face when you saw him—" This time she didn't even try to swallow the peal of laughter which bubbled up inside her.

Before it could quite reach the surface, however, Kurt's arm closed around her shoulders and pulled her off balance toward him. Suddenly, before Lissa realized what he intended, his lips brushed hers lightly and then settled into a firm kiss which, along with robbing her of any desire to laugh, took away the little breath control she still maintained.

His touch burned through her sweater, scorching her skin as easily as if she were wearing nothing at all. His mouth against hers was neither gentle nor soft. It was uncompromising, almost demanding—though not harsh.

For an instant time seemed to fold in on itself, and she was back in his room at the fraternity house. She was curled up on his bed because there was no other place big enough to spread out textbook, notebooks, scratch paper, calculator, and all the tools of the mathematician's trade. She was shifting around to get comfortable, trying to find a position that would support her back and still keep the books at an angle where both of them could see. Finally Kurt draped an arm around her shoulders and pulled her up next to him, propped against the pillows at the head of the narrow bed. She'd tensed at the idea of being so close to him, half-lying together on the single bed, and he'd joked about how rigid her muscles felt and then turned back to the problem she'd been demonstrating. He'd been so casual about it that he hadn't seemed to even notice that his arm was still around her. And it hadn't occurred to Lissa that he might have other plans....

Not until midway through her explanation, when she'd realized he wasn't looking at the notebook any longer but at her. As she'd stumbled to a halt he'd kissed her, and then, eyes narrowing, said that since it was clearly her first kiss he'd be happy to give her some pointers. And he'd kissed her again, very slowly and sensually, just to demonstrate step by step how it was done.

He'd been wrong and right, all at the same time. It had not been her first kiss, but it had been the first one that mattered. The first one that had warmed her, curled her toes, made her insides go mushy. The first one she hadn't wanted to end....

This time the kiss was different—not tentative, not exploratory. But it evoked the same rush of sensation in her, the same heat, the same intensity that had made her want, on that long-ago night, to learn just as much as he could teach her.

Get a grip, Lissa, she told herself. *Just because last time it ended up being a whole lot more than a kiss doesn't mean you want it to this time, not after last time.*

Still, it took more effort than she liked to admit to protest. Fighting off attraction, she had to admit, took just as much attention as did wallowing in it. But first she had to get control of her body—how had she ended up lying sprawled across the stairs, anyway? She planted her hand against Kurt's chest to push him away, and felt as if she'd succeeded only in welding them together with the heat he'd stirred deep within her.

Which simply proved, she told herself, that she had the normal range of hormones. It sure didn't have anything to do with Kurt himself, because she'd learned that lesson long ago.

"Knock it off, Callahan." Despite her best efforts she sounded breathless. "I thought I'd made myself clear that—"

From a few steps above them, a sultry feminine voice said, "I do so hate to interrupt such a touching scene, but if you'd excuse me so I could get through...."

Lissa's head snapped back so sharply that she felt the crack as a muscle popped in her neck. A few steps above them stood a dark-haired beauty, looking impossibly tall from this angle.

There hadn't been anyone in the hall or on the

stairs when Lissa had come out of the living room. Even though she'd been caught up in her amusement she remembered looking around to be certain it was safe to laugh. So how had this woman managed to come down without her hearing anything?

Stupid question, Lissa told herself. *You were a bit preoccupied just now.*

Lissa slid to one side of the stairs, and Kurt stood up. "Sorry to be in your way—Miss…?" he said.

"Oh, I quite understand. Seizing the moment and all that." The brunette slinked down the last few stairs and, once at floor level, smiled up at him and held out a languid hand. "I'm Mindy Meadows. Nice to meet you. I suppose you'll be coming back to join the party sometime, so I'll go in to sit with my mother now." Without a glance at Lissa, she drifted off into the living room.

"Mindy Meadows?" Kurt said slowly.

"Marian's daughter? Not her little friend."

"The precise relationship doesn't make much difference. I will now accept your apology."

Lissa was aghast. "*My* apology? For *what?*"

"For not taking all this seriously, for starters."

"Oh, come on, Kurt. Like you can't avoid unwanted attention. If there are really so many women after you, why hasn't one of them nailed you yet?"

"And for assuming I was wrong about Ray—"

"You *were* wrong about Ray!"

"I erred in details, not in substance."

"Gender's a bit more than a detail. Stop trying to change the subject. Whatever you were trying to prove with that kiss, give it up. You're not going to get anywhere."

He sat down beside her once more. "Really? I thought I'd gotten quite a long way." His gaze roved over her with a warmth that made her want to slap him. "I certainly proved that it would be no great hardship for you to play along and pretend. But if it makes you uncomfortable…."

Something warned her not to agree.

"Then I'd have to wonder why."

"Because you don't need protection."

He shot a look toward the living room, as if he could see Mindy through the wall.

"You're doing it again, Kurt—acting as if there couldn't possibly be a woman in the world who's indifferent to you."

"Mindy doesn't fall into that category."

"I suppose your psychic powers tell you that? Well, I'm not going to indulge you." She pushed herself up from the step. She was still a little wobbly, she noted. "I'm going back to the party. Since I'm *not* going to be playing the role of your girlfriend, I might as well get a closer look at Ray."

Lissa had less than no interest in Ray. All she really wanted to do was escape—or perhaps go jump off

Kurt's climbing wall at the mere idea that he could affect her so much with a kiss.

But of course that hadn't just been a kiss—not an ordinary kiss. It had brought back memories she'd tried for six years to suppress, of the kiss that had changed her life.

It had not been her first kiss, but it had been the first one that mattered. The first one that had warmed her, curled her toes, made her insides go mushy. The first one she hadn't wanted to end....

So of course it hadn't ended. Lissa took full responsibility for that fact, because she could have stopped him if she'd really wanted to. She could have swatted him across the chin and walked out.

Instead, she had let the kiss go on, deeper and deeper, long past enjoyment and into hunger. Hunger that she had thought—if she'd been thinking at all by then—was shared. She'd let herself believe that it was as important to him as it had been to her.

By then she'd had no control left at all. She not only couldn't have stopped him, she couldn't stop herself. And so for the first time in her life she had let her inhibitions be stroked away by a man's touch on her body, and she had let Kurt Callahan make love to her.

Ultimately, a long time later, she'd come back to her senses. She'd been embarrassed to find herself wrapped around him, clinging, almost begging. Mortified at the idea of being naked and exposed where his roommate might walk in. Ashamed by the depth of a passion she'd never suspected she possessed. Abashed to remember everything she'd done and everything she'd let him do. Disconcerted to realize that the thing she wanted most just then was to do it all over again.

And horrified by the stunned expression on Kurt's face. It had taken her a while to realize that he was just as dazed as she was, but for entirely different reasons. Like an idiot, she'd asked what he was thinking—and when he'd said something about her being a whole lot different than he'd expected, the shock in his voice had brought her back to earth with a bang.

It had become apparent that he, too, had gotten much more than he'd bargained for—but in a whole different way. He was, she'd thought, clearly afraid that now he wouldn't be able to get rid of her.

"I guess I'd better be going," she'd said, and when he hadn't argued the point she'd pulled herself together and made her escape. She remembered being quite proud of the fact that her voice hadn't even trembled as she'd stood in the doorway of his room and said she'd see him later.

She'd gone to calculus class the next day, still sensitive about how much of herself she'd revealed to him, braced to greet him with cool civility, as if none of it had happened. If it hadn't been important to him, then she'd make sure he understood that it hadn't been important to her, either.

But before she'd even made it to the lecture hall the whispers had started, and the truth had quickly become clear. He had placed a bet on her...and it was plain that his bet had paid off. So when she'd come face to face with him at the classroom door at the end of the lesson, she'd cut him dead and walked away.

It had hurt for a while. Quite a while, if she was honest. But in the end she'd chalked it up to experience. She hadn't just gotten a college credit for that calculus class, she'd earned the equivalent of a graduate degree in human relations.

But it was long over. Not important anymore. And now—well, now she'd positively enjoy watching Kurt get caught in the same kind of manipulation he'd created for her.

The innocence of the woman, Kurt fumed, not to see with a glance what Mindy Meadows was. Or perhaps Lissa had seen the woman quite clearly and was simply looking forward to the show.

Kurt swore under his breath and reached for Lissa's coat, still draped across the bannister, to hang it up. The wide oak boards at the foot of the stairs where their feet had rested were wet with the half-melted snow they'd tracked in. No—snow that *he'd* tracked in. Lissa had kicked off her shoes the instant they'd come in the door; he remembered thinking that she was acting as if she felt right at home in his grandmother's house.

At any rate, he'd better mop up the mess before Janet saw it, or there would be hell to pay. He took off his own shoes, hung up the coats, and went to the kitchen for paper towels.

Janet was rolling out pastry, muttering under her breath. "'Just make a few snacks for the guests,' she says. If I'd known she was going to have a party I'd have laid in supplies. I'm the one who'll look bad if I can't come up with something fancy."

"Don't try. Put out stale pretzels and maybe they'll go home early and give us all a break." He pulled a wad of paper towels off the roll.

Janet glowered. "Live Christmas trees, spur-of-the-moment decorating parties.... Mrs. Wilder never did this sort of thing before that woman came. She's bewitched, your grandmother is—that's what's going on. She's not acting like her normal self at all."

Bewitched....

That was putting it a little strongly, of course. But there was no denying that Lissa had a strange effect on people. Even Kurt himself.

Not that he was completely crazy where Lissa was concerned. He had good reason for proposing a truce and a mock courtship. A mild flirtation, the occasional longing look, perhaps a meaningful clasp of the hands—that would be enough to ward off approaches by the Mindys of the world. Lissa had proved it, in the store just this morning.

But then she'd laughed at the whole idea—a laugh which was no less musical and infectious even when she'd been practically choking herself to hold it in—and he'd lost all sense of proportion. He'd certainly never intended to do anything like what had actually happened in the front hall just now. Stretching her out on the staircase as if it were a bed…as if he were still a randy frat boy with a girl in his room and a necktie on the doorknob….

Janet was looking at him keenly. "What's she been doing to you?"

"Nothing at all," Kurt said airily.

You're a liar, his conscience whispered. *Ever since you saw her again, you've been wondering whether she really did kiss like an angel all those years ago. And now that you know, what are you going to do about it? Start trying to find out if she still makes love that way, too? Hardly.*

"Well, you'd better keep your head, or you'll wake up one morning and not know what hit you. I'm talking about things like lawyers."

The change of direction was so unexpected that Kurt started to laugh. "How did lawyers get into this?"

"I don't know," Janet said primly. "I just heard that woman suggest to your grandmother that the next step she needed to take was to talk to her lawyer."

Well, he'd always suspected that Janet listened at keyholes. Nevertheless, the whole idea sobered him. What the hell did his grandmother need to discuss with a lawyer, anyway? And even if she did, why would Lissa be the one suggesting it? She was a juvenile accountant, not a budding attorney.

Janet slapped the pastry down on a baking sheet and waved it at him. "You're between me and the oven."

Kurt wiped up the puddle at the foot of the stairs, tossed the paper towels into the nearest wastebasket, and headed for the living room.

Though he was walking as he did when in the woods—trying not to make a sound because it startled the animals—it was apparent that Mindy had been watching for him. The instant he saw her face she was already starting to smile in his direction. He wondered if she had a crick in her neck from keeping her head turned toward the doorway all the time he'd been gone. And, as far as that went, how could he possibly have thought that the way Lissa had looked at him that night at the cloakroom counter had been a predatory gaze? Here was the real thing, and there was no comparison.

Mindy was on one side of the tree, holding up a glossy ornament and looking past it toward him. She was probably checking out her reflection from the corner of her eye, Kurt thought. Making sure there wasn't a crumb stuck to her upper lip.

But it was the tableau on the other side of the tree which captured his attention. Ray was holding two bright red bricks in each hand, displaying them triumphantly like a weightlifter. The guy was posing for Lissa, and, sure enough, she was soaking it up. He wondered if she was really attracted or if she was doing it just to get his goat—to pay Kurt back for that kiss in the hallway.

"They're for the stockings, dear," his grandmother was saying.

"Bricks?" Lissa sounded doubtful. "I thought that was coal."

"Not to put *in* the stockings. The bricks are to weigh the tops on the mantel, so the stockings won't come tumbling down when Santa fills them."

Lissa looked thoughtful, as if the idea of a stocking packed so full that gravity might have an impact was something she'd never contemplated before.

Was that shadow in her eyes just a trick of the light, or did she really look sad? Kurt wondered if she even owned a Christmas stocking. If, in fact, she'd *ever* had a stocking....

Don't even start thinking of that pathetic little tree and how woebegone it looked, he told himself. *You'll only get yourself in deeper trouble.*

The *maître d'* in charge of the hotel dining room greeted Kurt soberly. "We don't see enough of you these days, Mr. Callahan. Your grandmother has her favorite table. Would you like me to show you over?"

"No, thanks—I remember." Which was not exactly a feat, considering that he'd been coming to

Sunday brunch here with his grandmother for years on his summer visits. Certainly since he was old enough to appreciate ice cream sundaes with all the trimmings, even if he hadn't yet learned to enjoy crab, sushi, quiche, or a good many of the hotel's other specialties. What astounded Kurt was that even if he turned up just once a year the *maître d'* called him by name. Did the guy have a notebook of mugshots tucked under the reservations calendar?

He forgot the *maître d'* as he approached the table. His grandmother was nowhere in sight, but Lissa was sitting with her back to him. Beyond the arched curve of the chair he could see only that she was wearing some kind of black sweater thing that hugged her figure. Her hair, short as it was, was upswept today, in a style that might have made anyone else look like they'd stuck a finger in an electrical socket. Lissa, on the other hand, looked as if she were wearing a flaming tiara. And between the hair and the high collar of the sweater a bit of the back of her neck, porcelain-ivory and delectable, peeked out and seemed to beckon to him.

Kurt wondered what she'd do if he slipped up behind her and dropped a kiss on that tempting spot just above her nape. Shove a seafood fork into him, most likely. In any case, it wasn't as if Marian and Mindy and Ray were around, needing to be impressed, so he'd be far better off keeping his hands—and lips—off. Besides, he had things to talk about with this young woman, and kissing the nape of her neck would only distract him.

Lissa looked up. "You're a bit late. Busy at the grand opening?"

"It's even crazier than yesterday was." He pulled out a chair beside her. "Actually, I'm surprised you're on time, with the mess you were in when I left this morning."

"Oh, it's still a mess. I just walked out and left it. That's the only house I've ever seen which has a linen closet the size of a bedroom."

"Wait till you get to the attic. There are built-in cedar-lined chests up there. What does she keep in the linen closet, anyway?"

Lissa gave him a gamine grin. "Linens, of course. There are towels in every color of the rainbow—and most of them have never been used. She still has the ones she got for her silver wedding anniversary. Did you know they used to package towels wrapped up in coordinating satin ribbon inside the boxes, with little bows and everything?"

"Towels come in boxes? I figure I'm doing well if they get onto the rack instead of the floor."

"If I find any that are already mildew-colored, I'll save them for you," Lissa said dryly.

"Very thoughtful. Where's Gran?"

"Trying to decide whether she's going to have breakfast first or just start with the seafood, I think."

"Good. I want to talk to you."

"Kurt, if you're going to start up that business about Ray and Mindy again—"

"Nope. I want to talk about lawyers. Why did you suggest to Gran that she needs one?"

Lissa hesitated and looked past him. Kurt was almost disappointed. He'd expected her to have an easy answer, even if—*especially* if—it wasn't quite a real one.

His grandmother had paused beside the table, resting a hand on his shoulder to keep him from rising. "I saw you come in, Kurt, but the chef was telling me how he makes his remoulade, and I didn't think I should just walk away in the middle of such an impassioned and poetic description."

She'd seen him come in? It was a very good thing, then, that he'd suppressed that urge to kiss Lissa's neck. Not that it had been anything more than a fleeting thought, he reassured himself. He'd never seriously contemplated acting on it.

"Don't just sit there—let's eat," his grandmother said cheerfully.

"What's it going to be?" Kurt asked. "Breakfast or seafood?"

"Neither. It occurred to me that life is short, so I'm going straight for the dessert bar and see how much I can pile on a plate." She marched off across the ballroom.

Kurt got himself a Belgian waffle, loaded with cream and picture-perfect fresh strawberries and blueberries. Lissa, he noted, had filled a plate with steamed seafood. It was probably not the sort of thing that came her way frequently, he thought—and told himself not to let sympathy get in the way of good sense. He looked over his shoulder and, not seeing his grandmother, started in again. "Tell me about the lawyer, Lissa."

This time she didn't even pause. He was annoyed with himself for giving her time to think. He'd handed her an opportunity to come up with a good story.

"Maybe you didn't know that your grandfather's name is still on the deed for the house? Hannah's isn't."

Kurt choked on his coffee. "It can't be. He's been dead for thirty years."

"It probably hasn't been any trouble all this time, but I thought she should get legal advice before she tried to dispose of a house that she technically doesn't own. It will be easier to work out the fine points beforehand rather than when there's someone impatiently waiting to move in."

He couldn't exactly argue with that. Still…. "You know, I can't quite see that subject coming up in casual conversation."

Lissa shrugged. "She thought it might be a problem, so she asked me."

"Then why hasn't she done something about it before now?"

"Because it was too much trouble. Haven't you

noticed how good she is at starting projects and then not finishing? There are half-made crafts and half-knitted sweaters all over the house, and— Here she comes."

His grandmother had been as good as her word. Kurt had never seen so much whipped cream on one plate. He ate his waffle slowly and thoughtfully. Janet had said the lawyer had been Lissa's idea, but from Lissa's description it sounded as if his grandmother had been the one to broach the subject. He wondered which was closer to the truth.

When Hannah finished the last bite of her peach cobbler and went back for seconds, Lissa watched her go out of sight and then said calmly, "I also suggested that she get legal advice and talk to an accountant about setting up a trust for Janet. But apparently by the time we got to that subject Janet had stopped listening."

"You knew she was eavesdropping?"

"I wouldn't call it eavesdropping. She was clearing the breakfast table at the time."

So Janet hadn't been listening at the keyhole after all. And if Lissa had been talking openly, knowing quite well that the housekeeper was there—well, that put an entirely different light on things.

Unless she was far more cunning than he'd given her credit for.... "A trust for Janet?" he asked.

"To provide some security for her in retirement."

"Janet's retiring?"

"What did you expect her to do?" Lissa said dryly. "Sign up at the employment agency for a new position?"

"No, I expected her to go with Gran."

Lissa shook her head. "In the retirement village everything will be provided. Hannah won't need a housekeeper or a cook—that's the whole point of the place—so Janet would be like a fifth wheel."

"So Gran *is* going to a retirement village? The last I knew you were insisting that she intended to move in with me."

"Perhaps she thought with Mindy around she'd be in the way."

"Don't threaten me with Mindy. I'm going to get something else. Should I bring you another plate of crab and shrimp, or would you like them just to wheel the cart over here?"

She didn't take offense. "I am being a bit of a pig, aren't I? I think I'll have a salad next, and then one of those cream puffs that Hannah obviously liked so well."

"Have two—they're small." When he returned with a plate of rare roast beef and all the accompaniments, his grandmother was nowhere to be seen. Kurt looked around in puzzlement. "Gran didn't go back to the dessert table for thirds—did she?"

"She hasn't come back at all." Lissa's eyebrows drew together. "I was watching for her while I was at the salad bar. I thought she'd probably just stopped to talk to a friend, but I hadn't realized how long she's been gone. Kurt, what if she's had another dizzy spell?"

"Possibly brought on by an overload of whipped cream," Kurt said dryly. "I doubt it. If she'd collapsed, we'd have heard the uproar."

"But if she felt faint and got herself to the ladies' room…." She was out of her chair. "I'll check."

But she'd taken only a couple of steps when the *maître d'* approached, a folded sheet of stationery in his hand. "Mr. Callahan, your grandmother asked me to deliver this to you."

"Does she need help?" Lissa asked anxiously.

Kurt opened the note. "Apparently not. She says she needs to do some shopping and she'll take a taxi home when she's done."

"I thought she was dead set against taxis?"

"Only when it suits her purpose, I suspect. She goes on to say: *And if you're wondering why I don't have Lissa drive me, it's because it's Lissa I'm shopping for. Have a good time, children. And don't miss the peach cobbler.*" He dropped the note on the table. "No wonder she had dessert first."

"I wonder where she went. I could still catch her, maybe."

"If you can figure out where to look. There must be a half-dozen department stores and a couple of hundred shops within six blocks of here. Relax and enjoy your salad. She doesn't want you."

"She hired me to drive her around."

"Apparently you get a day off for good behavior. What's the matter, really? Don't you like gifts? For somebody who's as nuts as you are about Christmas—"

"Not from her," Lissa said. "I mean—of course I like to get things. But she doesn't need to buy me anything. She's already given me a wonderful gift."

He was taken aback for an instant. Then he realized that of course she didn't mean anything material. He couldn't help but wonder, however, exactly what it was that Lissa saw as the "wonderful gift" Gran had given her. He listed the possibilities in his head. Two weeks away from that frightful boarding house, a salary which he suspected would be far above her normal pay, an old-fashioned Christmas with food and decorations galore....

"What did she give you?" he asked idly. "The SUV?"

Her gaze froze him in his chair. He wondered how anything as friendly and warm as her eyes could turn to icicles without warning.

"Thanks for reminding me," Lissa said. "Since I have a vehicle at my disposal, I don't have to stick around for this sort of treatment. And I have an errand to run. Excuse me, please." She pushed her salad away.

Kurt put out a hand. As his fingers brushed her wrist he could feel the surge of her anger like an electrical charge. "Stop. Lissa, I apologize. I shouldn't have said that."

She stayed in her chair, but she looked like a bird perched on a wire, ready to fly. "You've already had one chance to be nice today. Why should I give you another one?"

He looked at her with the most endearing expression he could manage. "Because I'll bring you a cream puff."

Lissa laughed. "You're an idiot."

"Yes. But I'm a charming one. What's the errand?"

She had relaxed enough to pick up her fork again. "I've got the first load of sheets and towels to drop off at the homeless shelter downtown."

"That's in a rough neighborhood."

"Not much worse than the one I live in."

He frowned. "And those people are addicts and ex-convicts—"

"Who know perfectly well that they have to behave or they'll get thrown out."

"It's the ones who *aren't* in the shelter who worry me. Driving a brand-new expensive SUV through that kind of territory is asking for trouble."

"At least I don't have to worry about a flat tire," Lissa pointed out. "And before you start ragging on me because I was originally planning to take Hannah along this afternoon, believe me—she'd have been under orders to stay in the car with the doors locked."

Somewhat to his surprise, that aspect hadn't occurred to him. He finished his roast beef. "I'll go with you."

She looked startled. "That's not necessary. You have a car here."

"I'll come back and pick it up."

"I was going to stop at my place for a minute. It's almost on the way."

"So we'll stop."

"You need to get back to work."

"This store will run all next year without me in the building. It can survive for an hour right now. But one thing's non-negotiable."

She looked doubtful.

"I'm driving," Kurt said. "Do you still want that cream puff, or are you ready to go?"

CHAPTER SIX

LISSA COULDN'T BELIEVE she'd agreed to let him come along. What had happened to her, anyway? Had a mere couple of days of the softer life made her less resilient, less self-sufficient? Surely she wasn't afraid. She walked all over campus and through a less than stellar neighborhood at all hours of the day and night. Why hadn't she just told him she could handle this by herself?

At any rate, if she'd felt the need for a bodyguard Kurt wouldn't have been her first choice. Oh, his muscles were impressive, and so was his agility—if she'd needed a reminder of that, seeing him on the climbing wall would have done the trick nicely—but he wasn't the bruiser type. He so obviously preferred charm to brawn as a method of getting his own way....

It might be amusing, though, to see how he handled himself in a squabble. Not that there was going to be one.

She also had to admit that it was also just plain nice to have an extra pair of hands as he supervised the unloading of the SUV while she filled out the donation forms. The whole thing took less than fifteen minutes.

As they pulled away from the shelter, Lissa said, "You see? I didn't need a bouncer along after all."

"Maybe not. But there's no telling what might have happened if I hadn't been there."

"Are you in training for the Olympic competition for largest ego, or what?"

"There's a medal for that?"

"I wouldn't doubt it—and you don't even need to practice. You're a shoo-in."

His smile made her want to reach out and flick a fingertip across the dimple in his cheek. "What are you going to tackle next?"

Lissa found herself frowning. "I'm not sure. Hannah hasn't given me any kind of agenda, and she seems to have gotten distracted by the whole Christmas thing. She spent the morning putting together Christmas baskets for me to mail tomorrow. And she wouldn't even have thought of the linen closet if I hadn't finally tackled her and demanded that she put me to work."

"It just occurs to me to wonder—if the linen closet's empty...."

"It's not, actually. There's another whole load to take to the women's shelter."

"Gran owed *two* entire carloads of sheets and towels? Do you want to take care of that right now?"

Lissa shook her head. "I know the director, so I'll take things there tomorrow—I don't get a chance to talk to her very often anymore. Besides, you can't help with that one because they don't allow men on the premises."

"Why not?"

"Because so many of the women are there because of violent men, that's why."

"Oh. Of course. Where is she coming up with these charities? Throwing darts at the phone book? Or is it you who's making the list? If you know the director—"

"I know lots of people—and there is the little matter of matching up what Hannah has to give away with what clients can actually use."

"Well, that should keep you entertained for a while. If the linen closet's going to be empty, does this mean I can't have clean sheets for the rest of my stay?"

"Of course you can," Lissa said heartily. "You can wash the ones that are on your bed anytime you like. Washer and dryer are in the basement."

He slanted a look at her. "Don't make the mistake of thinking I can't do my own laundry."

"But will your things still be the same color when they come out of the washer as when they went in? Seriously, Kurt—when was the last time you were in that basement?"

"I don't know. A few years, probably."

"Well, neither your grandmother nor Janet should be running up and down those stairs. I tried to stop Hannah from taking a load of laundry down this morning, and she said she'd been doing it for as long as she could remember and she intended to keep right on."

The silence stretched out. Lissa had almost concluded that Kurt wasn't going to answer, when he said, "She intends to keep on? You think she's starting to waver about moving?"

"Maybe," Lissa said slowly. "It's one thing to give away sheets and towels you've never taken out of the box, but from here on the decisions will only get harder. It may take her longer than I expected. You're sure you don't mind stopping by the boarding house?"

Kurt shook his head and turned toward her old neighborhood.

He might not mind stopping, Lissa thought, but *she* certainly minded. If she hadn't forgotten her address book in her hurried move she wouldn't have gone anywhere near the place. Not until she had to.

In fact, she realized the instant they walked in, though the boarding house hadn't changed at all, spending two days away from the gloomy atmosphere had made it seem even worse than usual. Dark and dingy, the hallway smelled of one of the residents' sausage and garlic lunch. She tried to hold her breath while she dug for her key.

"What are we picking up?" Kurt asked.

"Just my address book. I'll only be a minute. You can wait outside if you like." She pushed the sliding door open.

She remembered perfectly well pulling boxes out from under the futon she used as a bed, and then pushing them back. Perhaps she hadn't put them away as neatly as she'd thought. But as surely as the broken Christmas ornament had told her that someone had invaded her privacy before, the twinge in Lissa's gut told her that it had happened again.

"What's the matter?" Kurt asked.

"Somebody's been in here, looking around. It's not important." She was talking to herself as much as to him. "There's nothing left worth stealing."

"That doesn't mean it's not important to you."

"I guess when I come back I'll put a padlock on the door for when I go out." She dug through the pile of books on the end of the mantel and found her tattered address book. "Come on, let's go. I'll deal with this later."

But Kurt didn't budge. "Get your stuff. All of it."

"What?"

"Don't leave anything behind."

"You're being a little high-handed again, aren't you? It's really not your business—"

"Is the furniture yours?"

She glanced from the futon to the one worn chair. "No, thank heaven."

"Then we don't have to have it put into storage. We'll take the rest of your things today, so you don't have to come back here."

"And where do you suggest I go in a couple of weeks, when the new semester starts? At least this place has a window."

He wandered over to look. "And such a view. An alley and a row of trash cans. Tell you what, Lissa—I'll pay the rent on an apartment for you."

Lissa frowned at him, not quite sure what she was hearing. "Why?"

"You're graduating in the spring, right?"

With a sudden flash of wry humor, Lissa said, "Well, I've learned the hard way not to count on anything. But that's the plan, yes."

"Then I'll pay your rent till you graduate."

Big as the offer looked to her, it was peanuts to him. *So don't go getting crazy, Lissa—it's not like he's offering to set you up in a love-nest.* "So what's the catch? I suppose in return you want me to play games for Mindy's benefit."

"You really think that would be enough?" His voice was almost a drawl. "Six months' rent is a tidy sum. What are you offering in exchange?"

She noted that his dimple was showing, and she couldn't decide whether to be relieved that he was teasing or annoyed that he was laughing at the idea of them being lovers—at least for anything more than a one-night stand. "I'm not interested in having an affair with you, that's for sure."

His eyebrows raised slightly. "I don't recall offering one. But if that's what you'd like, Lissa…." His voice had gone low and soft, with a rough edge.

This was how he'd sounded that night. She'd never forgotten, and when she heard that tone again quivers started to run through her body, reminding her of emotions and sensations that were far better left buried. She tried to ignore them. "Now if you'd forget about the apartment and hire me to do an internship at your store instead…."

"What for?"

At least now he was taking her seriously, she noted. The dimple had vanished. "Because in order to get a good job when I graduate I need to have experience in the field. But most internships are unpaid."

"And you can't afford to give up the job you have now."

She held out both hands, her gesture encompassing the dingy little room. "It's because I insist on being surrounded by such luxury, you see."

"Yeah, if you'd just cut back on your standard of living…."

"And I can't do both jobs and keep up with my classes, too. So—"

"I've got it. If you share a place with someone…."

"Like who? You?"

"There you go again—tempting me. And you say you're not interested in an affair."

"Kurt, the only way you'd be interested in a roommate is if there was a revolving door on your bedroom."

"Damn, you have good ideas." He sobered. "All right, Lissa. Here's the deal. Originally, you thought that within two weeks Gran would change her mind about clearing out the house. I'm raising the stakes. You get her to settle down to this project and get it over with, and I'll fork over your rent for the next six months. And I'll think about that internship."

Was he serious about giving her a job? Lissa shook her head in disbelief. "You want me to have the whole house cleared in two weeks? I don't think it can be done."

"Nope. I want her to make that decision you're so sure she'll reach—either to keep the house and leave everything right where it is or call an auctioneer. I really don't care which she ends up doing."

"Because either way she'll be done with it?"

"Yes. All I care about is that she not kill herself by trying to clear out all the debris she's collected in sixty-odd years."

"Isn't there anything in all that so-called debris that you care about, Kurt? Souvenirs? Mementoes?" She was honestly curious. "You spent every summer in that house when you were growing up—isn't there a single thing there you want?"

"Now that you mention it…."

Suddenly she realized that he was standing closer to her than she'd expected. He was right behind her at the mantel, so close that she could feel the warmth of his chest against her spine. His hands skimmed her shoulders and moved down her arms, and he turned her to face him.

"One thing does come to mind," he said softly.

He was so close that there was barely room to take a breath. So close that she couldn't even smell the sausage drifting in from the hallway anymore, only the light scent of his aftershave. She couldn't stop herself from looking at his mouth. She couldn't quite suppress her quick intake of breath as she looked. And she couldn't prevent the very tip of her tongue from running along her upper lip.

His eyes narrowed. Slowly, and very deliberately, he lowered his head.

She felt like bacon being held over a hot griddle—feeling the heat, knowing that very soon she would be sizzling out of control. A little shiver ran through her.

"What was that?" he whispered. "Not revulsion, I'm sure. Are you scared? Or eager?"

She opened her mouth, not quite knowing what she'd say. But before she could try to form words he took advantage of what must have looked like willingness and kissed her.

His caress was soft, almost tender. The very gen-

tleness of it fed her hunger, made her want more—
and, as if he tasted her desire, his kiss grew more
demanding. His hands slipped to her back and drew
her closer, until she was melting against him,
meeting him kiss for kiss.

What are you doing? Lissa asked herself.

She'd been so certain that she could handle him
now, that their single night together had been an
anomaly, that she'd only been so vulnerable to him
back then because she was young and inexperienced. Even that stolen kiss on the stairway didn't
really count in the equation, she'd told herself,
because it had taken her by surprise. But once
warned she had been on her guard. He shouldn't be
affecting her like this.

But all he had to do was touch her, and she went to
pieces like a tarpaper shack in a hurricane. Obviously
she wasn't as experienced as she'd thought she was.

And, just as obviously, he was even more so. But
the most terrifying part about that, she realized,
was that when he was kissing her she didn't care
that Kurt's women came and went with about the
same frequency as the daily newspaper. She only
cared that right at this moment his attention was
entirely focused on her.

Maybe the moment is enough....

Hardly aware of what she was saying, she
murmured, "We're not in college anymore, Kurt."

"And that's the real beauty of it," he whispered

against her lips. "No more confusion. No more games."

No more bets....

"Just two people who know what they want."

With the last of her strength Lissa managed to break free. "Yes—and I also know what I don't want. I don't want this."

Kurt smiled. "Sure, Lissa," he said softly. "You just keep telling yourself you don't—and maybe someday you'll make yourself believe it. Now, let's get your stuff gathered up."

She didn't have the energy to battle him, and in any case, taking a few more of her belongings didn't mean she wasn't ever coming back. So, almost meekly, Lissa helped to load the rest of her possessions into the SUV. Then she dropped Kurt off to pick up his car and went straight back to Hannah's house, hoping to have all her things unloaded and safely tucked away in the guestroom before Hannah returned from her shopping trip. There was no sense in upsetting her hostess—which the news that Lissa was all but officially homeless was quite sure to do.

It took seven trips for Lissa to transfer all the stuff from the SUV upstairs. By the time she'd finished, the guestroom, with its solid furniture and luxurious drapes, looked like a warehouse.

As she came down the stairs the doorbell rang. Hannah was standing on the front porch, her eyes bright and her arms full of gift-wrapped boxes. "I couldn't reach my key," she said cheerfully. "In fact, I couldn't get to my wallet to pay the driver, so the poor man's still waiting out there for me to come back. Put these under the tree, will you?"

Lissa juggled the boxes into the living room, where the lights were gleaming on the Christmas tree. By the time she had them neatly stacked Hannah had come back from paying the taxi, dusting her hands together. "Did you and Kurt have a nice brunch?"

"You scared us to death, you know, disappearing like that."

"But not for long, I hope. I just asked Henry to wait until I was safely out the door before he delivered my note."

"I think he gave you an extra-long headstart. It looks as if you finished up your shopping list."

"Don't you want to know which ones are yours?"

"Which *ones?* Plural? Hannah—"

"And now I'm ready for tea." Hannah smiled and dived into the pile of packages. "I got Janet a gadget that's just too good to save for her stocking. She can use it while she's cooking the Christmas turkey."

Just what we need. One more gadget to clear out when it comes time to tackle the kitchen. "I'm sure she'll be thrilled," Lissa said.

There were two voices in the kitchen, pitched softly but still quite audible. One was Janet, of course; the other was deeper. Lissa hadn't seen the Jaguar outside, so Kurt must have come in while she was making the last trip upstairs and settling her belongings.

Lissa paused for an instant just outside the swinging door. It had been difficult enough to work with Kurt after that kiss this afternoon, loading up the SUV and then taking him back to the hotel. To face him in front of an audience….

Well, there was no help for it. She put her hand on the door just as Janet spoke.

"She brought in a lot more stuff today," the housekeeper said. "Strange-looking stuff."

"I know." Kurt's voice was casual. "There was a problem with the place she lives in."

"Kurt's home already," Hannah said, and the voices in the kitchen stopped abruptly.

Hannah greeted Kurt with a kiss on the cheek and handed Janet a long thin box. "It's a special fork," she said. "It reads the temperature instantly when you stick it into a roast or a turkey."

"The old-fashioned way is good enough for me," Janet muttered. "Sit down. I'll get you some tea."

Hannah pulled out a chair at the kitchen table, opposite Kurt. Between them, stacked on the gleaming oak surface of the table, were a dented stockpot, a rusty cookie sheet, and a glass cake pan with a big chip out of the corner. "What are these for, Janet?"

"They're things we don't need anymore," the housekeeper said.

"And neither does anyone else, I'd say." Hannah sounded quite cheerful about it. "Isn't that cake pan likely to explode if it's heated again, with that crack in it? Put them in the garbage, Janet, not the donation pile."

Lissa was just concluding with relief that Hannah's hearing hadn't been quite good enough for her to distinguish the words they'd overheard, when Hannah went on, "What's the problem with your apartment, Lissa?"

It was Kurt who answered. "The thieves hit again."

"Oh, no, my dear! What did they take this time?"

"Nothing," Lissa said.

"But of course you don't feel secure leaving your possessions there." Hannah pushed the stockpot aside so Janet could set a cup of tea in front of her. "You brought all your things, of course? Good. You can stay here just as long as you like."

Kurt shifted in his chair. "You won't be here, Gran."

"Oh, Kurt, I won't be ready to move anytime soon. I've been just too busy with other things. Lissa can drive the sieve to her classes when they start up again, and then we can take our time with the cleaning." She sounded delighted.

Kurt's gaze met Lissa's. The message in his eyes was quite clear—*Remember our deal.*

Lissa smothered a sigh. Suddenly the next couple

of weeks didn't look quite so much like a holiday. And as for the chance of an internship—she might as well kiss that goodbye right now.

Maximum Sports was not nearly as busy on Monday afternoon as it had been over the weekend, though the crowd was still respectable. Lissa couldn't believe the sheer size of the place; she and Hannah had obviously covered only a fraction of it on Saturday. But then, she recalled, almost the first thing which had caught her eye that day was Kurt hanging off the ridiculous wall—and after that she'd barely seen anything else until he was safely down.

Only because it would have been too awful if he'd fallen and gotten hurt in front of his grand-mother, she told herself.

Again this time her gaze went straight to the wall, but since it was apparent that neither of the climbers was Kurt—one seemed to be no more than a child, the other was very blond—she relaxed and went looking for him.

Twice she had to stop a salesclerk to ask for directions, and she felt as if she'd walked a mile or two before she finally found Kurt at a kiosk toward the back of the store, flicking through pages on a computer screen. Figures and code numbers scrolled by at a pace almost too fast for her to see.

"Hey," she said. "Figuring out how good the grand opening sales were?"

He looked up. "It's hard to tell, with Christmas mixed in."

"Well, math never was your strong suit. Want me to take a look?"

He surveyed her for a long moment without answering.

It had been a careless offer, and not one she had expected him to take up. But the long stare made Lissa feel defensive. "I am almost an accountant, after all," she pointed out. "And I'm not some corporate spy. Even if I saw something valuable in your data I wouldn't know who to sell it to."

Kurt pushed his tall stool back from the computer. "Be my guest."

It took Lissa a couple of minutes to untangle the details—things like how sales were reported and compared with the remaining inventory, and how the thirty-seven locations were coded. "It looks as if this store took in the most cash over the last seven days, but the Denver one is the most profitable."

"It's the oldest." His eyebrows had gone up. "You could tell that in just a few minutes?"

"It shouldn't have taken that long. I could simplify your reporting system."

"That's what you want to do for an internship?"

Lissa's nerves were thrumming—was he actually considering it? She forced a careless-looking shrug. "Depends on what you need."

"I'll keep that in mind. How did the battle end this morning?"

"The one over the breakfast table, about the pots and pans? I'd call it a draw. Janet insisted she needs to keep every item in the kitchen in order to cook a holiday dinner, and Hannah told her that after Christmas either Janet will clean out the cupboards properly or Hannah will send me in to do it."

"Good. Gran's getting serious about the cleaning out."

"Well, I couldn't say that, exactly. I offered to start on the attic this morning and she gave me a shopping list instead. That's why I'm here."

"Too bad. It doesn't sound like you're going to get your internship, does it?" He didn't sound sorry at all. "Unless—"

"*Not* interested."

"But you didn't even listen," he complained.

Lissa took a deep breath. This was going to be even tougher than she'd imagined. "Kurt, would you loan me some money?"

"Gran gave you a list of things to buy and no funds to do it with?"

"Of course not. But I'd like to get her something nice for Christmas, and until she pays me I don't have enough cash."

"Then ask her for an advance on your wages."

"So I can buy her a present? That would be tacky, Kurt."

"What's the difference between asking her for an advance against your first paycheck and asking me for a loan till you get paid? It's the same money."

She had to admit it was an excellent question.

"And you're supposed to be the accounting whiz." Kurt shook his head, almost sadly.

Lissa bit her lip and looked straight at him. "All right, I confess—no matter what I do, it's tacky. The trouble is, I don't have any more family heirlooms to pawn."

His gaze drifted over her. "I wouldn't be so certain of that."

Lissa glared at him.

"You still have that quilt."

The sudden change of direction left her speechless for an instant. "I'm surprised you remember the quilt. What's it worth to you?"

"I'm the one who doesn't appreciate heirlooms, remember?" He pulled out his money clip. "Keep the quilt. How much do you need?" He peeled a couple of bills out of his money clip.

"Not that much. And I'll consider the quilt to be security for my debt."

"I suppose I'll end up hiring you just so I can garnish your wages instead of ending up the owner of a quilt I don't want," Kurt grumbled.

She folded the money and pushed it deep into the pocket of her jeans. She should be feeling relieved that he hadn't made it hard on her, she thought. And yet…she knew that he'd read her mind and knew perfectly well what she was thinking. She'd expected him to proposition her in return for the loan. More in a teasing way than as a serious suggestion, of course. Instead, he'd shifted course like an America's Cup racer before the wind.

Because, though teasing her was fun, he wasn't about to let things get serious. Well, that certainly told her where she stood.

Kurt looked past her and stifled a groan.

Lissa looked over her shoulder to see Mindy and Ray coming toward them.

Mindy kissed the air in the vicinity of Lissa's cheek and sidled up to Kurt. "I've never been in one of your stores before," she gushed. "But I should have expected it would be just like you—you're so big and strong and impressive and solid."

And looking slightly sick to the stomach at the moment, Lissa would have added.

"I'm dying to try the climbing wall," Mindy went on.

I'll just bet you are.

"In fact, it took us so long to find you that by the time I get into my gear it'll be my turn on the wall. Would you like to come and join me?"

To her amazement, Lissa realized that it wasn't Kurt whom Mindy was inviting, but her.

"The guys can watch us," Mindy went on.

"Sorry," Lissa said. "I have some shopping to

do. In fact, I must be going—goodness, is that the time? I'll see you all later. I know—maybe we should all go out for dinner one night."

She couldn't stop herself from looking over her shoulder as she walked away. Kurt was watching her.

No doubt he was renewing his vow to strangle her, she thought, and with her good humor restored, she went off to look for the first item on Hannah's list.

Kurt watched as Lissa walked off. The vintage coat she wore was oversized for her, but it did nothing to hide her femininity. The coat swayed along with her hips, every bit as intriguingly as if she'd been wearing a fancy ballgown with a hoop skirt, and he'd bet that she knew it. At the very least she obviously realized he was watching her, for she not only looked back at him, but actually had the nerve to wink just before she went out of sight between two racks of fishing equipment.

Now, there's a fitting description, Kurt thought. *She's just one more lure, mixed in with the rest of the bait.*

Except he knew better. She wasn't just one more lure. She was the top of the line.

He'd known from the beginning that Lissa Morgan was trouble. Even before he'd actually recognized her he'd realized that much. And why he hadn't had the sense to run....

You did run, he reminded himself. *Well—almost. It wasn't your idea for her to actually move in.*

Still, he could have kept his distance. Instead, he'd managed to get himself even more entangled as the days went on. What had he been thinking?

Either she would succeed in her mission, and he would owe her an apartment, or she wouldn't— which meant she'd probably be hanging around Gran's house whenever he happened to be in Minneapolis. He wasn't sure which was worse. Her staying at the house, he supposed. Because he could rent her an apartment, pay for it in advance, and never set foot in it. Except he had his doubts it would be quite that easy to avoid her.

Because you don't want it to be easy, his conscience whispered.

Ever since Lissa had made that crack yesterday about the possibility of them having an affair, he hadn't been able to get the idea out of his mind. Not that he hadn't had a few unseemly thoughts even before that—but having his grandmother in the bedroom just under his had kept those pretty much under control. But the idea of an apartment, where the neighbors didn't care and there was no elderly bright-eyed woman to wonder what was going on…. Yes, as fantasies went, that one was a whole lot more interesting.

Mindy was watching him, he realized, with her eyes narrowed. Well, if she'd gotten the message that he was too interested in Lissa to pay attention to her that was all to the good. Especially because he hadn't had to say it, or do anything much to create the image. Or even talk Lissa into cooperating.

"Yes?" he said, as if he was having to pull himself back from a far country. "You said you'd reserved a climbing time? You'd better not take a chance of missing it. There's usually a waiting list for cancellations."

"I'll stick around," Ray offered. "I'd like to talk to you, Kurt."

"Sorry, I'm busy right now, or I'd love to chat. And you don't want to miss Mindy on the climbing wall—I bet it'll be quite a show." He shook hands with Ray.

"You mentioned dinner," Mindy said abruptly.

I didn't, Kurt wanted to point out. *Lissa did—and that's an entirely different thing.*

"It's a lovely idea, Kurt. Let's do it tonight. You're free, right, Ray?"

The question was careless, as if Ray's main responsibility was to be at Mindy's command. It didn't surprise Kurt that she'd want an extra man hanging around. The Mindys of the world were like that. But they usually weren't quite so obvious about it. Surely she didn't think Kurt would be jealous? Or perhaps she was just making sure that he realized that she wasn't serious about Ray. As if it would make a difference to him whether she was or not.

"Dinner?" Mindy said again.

"I'll have to check whether Lissa's made other plans, so—"

"It was her idea," Mindy pointed out.

And I'm going to get her for it, too. "Dinner," he agreed. "You choose the place."

Mindy named a restaurant. "They have the best lobster Newburgh I've ever eaten, and they can always fit me in with a reservation."

"Fine," Kurt said. "We'll pick you up at seven." Then he went back to staring at the computer terminal—not studying the inventory this time, but figuring out how to get even with Lissa for landing him with Mindy and Ray for an entire evening.

CHAPTER SEVEN

FILLING HANNAH'S SHOPPING list wasn't the end of the job, of course. When she got home, Lissa found her employer at the small table in the middle of the library, humming a carol as she wrapped boxes. "Oh, good, you can take over," Hannah said. "I believe my ankles are swelling, so it's past time for a break."

Lissa stacked her purchases neatly at the end of the table. "Swollen ankles? You assured me you'd see a doctor, Hannah."

"And I will. But swollen ankles are nothing unusual for me."

"This week."

"Well, I don't know when I'll be able to go in. It'll be hard to get an appointment right now—with the holiday so close, you know." Hannah nodded firmly, as if to deny there could be any disagreement with her point of view, and went off.

Relatively sure that—having gotten the last word—Hannah wouldn't come back for a while,

Lissa wrapped her gift first. It was a small package, and she took particular care that it be beautiful.

She had done almost no Christmas shopping for years—student budgets being what they were, she and her friends had long ago opted to give themselves a present by making Christmas a gift-free zone. It was funny, though, how quickly the knack came back—folding the heavy paper to make a crisp crease, keeping everything square and tight, curling the ribbon and adding just the right color bow to finish off the presentation. The stack of wrapped boxes grew steadily.

She made a trip to the living room to deposit the finished gifts under the tree, and realized that instead of sitting with her feet up Hannah was in the dining room, digging in the bottom of a built-in cabinet. The table was already stacked with old-fashioned pink vinyl cases—some round, some square.

Lissa went in to see what was going on. One of the cases had been unzipped and the top folded back. She peeked in to see a stack of glossy china plates—the color of heavy cream, rimmed with gold, with a soft pattern of pink roses at the edges.

They'd been using china for every meal—no inexpensive pottery for Hannah—but nothing to compare with this. "It's beautiful," Lissa said.

"It's my wedding china. I don't use it often, but I wanted to get it out for Christmas."

Lissa had no trouble hearing the part Hannah hadn't said. *Since it might be the last time.*

Hannah sighed. "I'd forgotten how much of it there is, and how much room it takes. I don't know what I'll do with all this."

Lissa looked at the long table, almost covered with vinyl cases. There must be enough china laid out there to serve sixteen—and it looked as if Hannah had all the extra pieces as well. She saw soup plates, serving bowls, coffeepots, cunning little covered dishes, even a cake stand. Hannah was quite right; there would not be room in the average retirement apartment for half of this.

But the answer was obvious—wasn't it? "I'm sure Kurt will want it," Lissa said. "After all, it's a family heirloom."

Hannah gave a genteel little snort. "Kurt lives in a shoebox," she said tartly. "And his idea of a nice plate is what you buy in the freezer section of the supermarket with the food already on it. He has no room or desire for anything sentimental."

"He won't always feel that way," Lissa argued. "He'll settle down someday."

"May I live so long. After the way his parents—" Hannah broke off. "It's been sixty years since I chose this pattern, and I haven't broken so much as a nut dish. Take my advice, Lissa—when you buy your china, get extras of everything. It's almost a guarantee that you'll never drop a single piece."

"I'll keep that in mind," Lissa said dryly. *When you buy your china....* As if that day would come anytime soon. She let the silence drag out until she couldn't bear it anymore, and then she tried to keep her voice casual. "What were you saying about Kurt's parents?"

Hannah didn't look up from the china. "Hmm? Oh, nothing—I was just talking to myself. Perhaps you're right. Someday he'll slow down enough to notice that women aren't just for entertainment, and material things aren't just junk."

The sadness which underlaid Hannah's tart tone tugged at Lissa's heart. But her sympathy was mixed with another sensation—the knowledge that, no matter how kindly Hannah was treating her and no matter how generous she was, she didn't consider Lissa to be anything more than an employee after all. She certainly wasn't like family.

And I never expected to be.

Still, it was a lesson worth remembering. It would be far too easy to forget her real place here, to believe that Hannah's kind treatment made Lissa something special, when in fact Hannah treated everyone that way.

"Sometimes," Hannah said softly, "it seems like it's just too much work to do this."

Here's your chance, Lissa told herself. "You don't have to do it all yourself, you know."

"Oh, my dear, I realize what a help you've been. I couldn't possibly have gotten so far in just a few days without you."

But we've barely scratched the surface, Lissa thought. "I don't mean me. There are auction companies—they'll come in and clear everything out, make arrangements—"

"And sell it all to the highest bidder."

There was no gentler way to put it. "Well, yes."

Hannah shook her head. "I hate the thought of an auction. All that sing-song talk, people yelling bids and pawing through things, hoping to get a bargain, dealers just wanting to make a profit…."

"You wouldn't have to be there to see it."

"I'd know it was going on."

Lissa considered, and then said carefully, "If it's the idea of an auction that bothers you, I've read about companies that offer tag sales instead. You could go ahead and move, and then they'd just take over the house and have a sort of gigantic garage sale of everything that's left."

She was so caught up in the idea that it took her a minute to realize that Hannah had gone even quieter than usual. "No," she said firmly. "Giving my belongings away is one thing, especially when they go to someone who needs them or who will appreciate them. But selling them—no. I couldn't stand to put a price tag on my china."

"I understand," Lissa said. "I have some precious

things of my own. Like a quilt my grandmother had just finished when she died."

"Really? I'd like to see it."

Lissa wondered if that was true, or if Hannah was grasping at any way to change the subject. "I'll bring it down later, if you like."

"What about right now? I'm at a standstill here, and I'm ready for a glass of sherry."

In truth, Lissa was glad to escape for a minute. She needed a break from the weight of emotion in the room every bit as much as Hannah did.

Kurt was coming in the side door as Lissa started up the stairs. She leaned over the bannister and beckoned to him, and as he came closer she caught the fragrance of his aftershave. The scent—along with the memories it evoked of the way he'd kissed her yesterday—made her almost dizzy. She clung to the bannister. "Whatever you do, don't suggest she auction off the china," she said under her breath. "In fact, if you're smart, you'll tell her you're wild about her china, you always have been, and you can't wait to own it."

Kurt looked up at her as if she'd been speaking Swahili. "You mean those dishes with the pink cabbage leaves on them?"

"It's Havilland china, and they're roses."

"Never saw a rose that looked like that before. What's been going on?"

"Let's just say that my suggestion of an auctioneer didn't go over well. I'll tell you later. We don't want her thinking we're conspiring."

"Even though we are? Relax—she'll just think we're flirting in the dark corners."

Lissa remembered the almost-sharp way Hannah had looked at her, and the way she'd dodged Lissa's question about Kurt's parents. "I don't think that would be much better," she muttered and went on upstairs.

By the time she came back, with the quilt in her arms, Kurt had poured his grandmother a sherry and had one waiting for Lissa as well. "I don't like what all this work is doing to you, Gran," he was saying as Lissa came in. "You look worried…awfully stressed. I talked to a friend who's in real estate today."

Lissa stopped in mid-step. With her hands full, she couldn't exactly wave her arms to get his attention, and jumping up and down would be a bit obvious. At any rate, he wasn't watching her; he was too intent on his mission.

"He'd like to come and take a look at the house sometime," Kurt went on. "He could give you an idea of what it might bring on the market, and then you'd have a better idea of—"

"No, thank you, Kurt." Hannah set her sherry glass down with a thump that threatened to shatter the crystal stem. "I need to speak to Janet for a moment. Excuse me, please."

"Well, that was certainly a brilliant stroke of diplomacy," Lissa said. She dropped the quilt in a heap at the end of the couch and planted her hands on her hips.

Kurt's jaw had sagged. He stared after Hannah for a moment, then turned to Lissa. "What did I say that was so awful?"

"You told her that you think the easiest way to get rid of everything she owns is to sell it to the highest bidder."

"Well, it is," he said defensively.

"You know that, and I know that—but it's not just *stuff* we're talking about here. It's her memories. And since I just made the same mistake a few minutes ago...."

Kurt snapped his fingers and grinned. "I knew if I waited long enough, this would turn out to be your fault!"

"Thanks. I appreciate you giving me so much credit. Did you at least tell her you want her china?"

"What in the hell would I do with her china? Use it for target practice?"

"Are you *trying* to cause her a heart attack? Never mind." Lissa sank down beside the quilt, one fingertip absently tracing the wheel-like pattern.

"Is that my quilt?"

Lissa bristled. "Your quilt? I didn't sell it to you. In fact, you said you didn't want it."

"I'm coming to terms with the reality of the situation." He stretched out a hand. "I couldn't remember what it looked like."

"Too bad I didn't realize that—I could have substituted a less meaningful one and you'd never have known the difference. Anyway, I'll pay the loan back, Kurt—so don't get attached to my quilt. Did Mindy convince you to go climbing with her?"

"She didn't invite me."

"Really? Oh, I guess that makes sense. You could get a much better view of her figure from the ground than if you were up there with her, especially if she was wearing a skintight bodysuit. Was she?"

"Probably. I didn't go and watch, either. I figured dinner tonight was enough time to spend paying attention to Mindy."

"Dinner? She actually went for the bait?"

"It was *your* idea, Lissa."

"Kurt, she knew perfectly well it was a *let's-do-lunch* sort of invitation—you know, the kind of thing you say when you absolutely don't mean it. Oh, I suppose she arranged it to be just the two of you? Poor Ray. Have a good time."

"I said we'd pick them up at seven."

"*We?*"

"You're not getting out of this, Lissa. You're going to dinner, too."

Hannah had come back in. "A dinner date? Who's going?"

"Ray and Mindy, Lissa and me."

Lissa saw her chance and seized it. "Unless you object, Hannah?" she said smoothly. "It's awfully late notice to leave you on your own, and I wouldn't want to hurt Janet's feelings by walking out on the meal she's prepared."

She tried to ignore Kurt's sardonic smile.

"Don't worry about Janet," Hannah said. "She's making a casserole that always tastes better the second day, so we'll just have it tomorrow instead. And as for me—all this rich food might be why my ankles are swelling. I'll make up for it by just having a boiled egg on a tray in front of the television tonight. I'll tell Janet you two won't be at home for dinner." She popped out of the room again, calling the housekeeper's name.

"That seems to settle it," Kurt said.

"Not necessarily. I can boil an egg for myself, Kurt."

"In Janet's kitchen? You must be joking. Besides…." He held out both hands, as if he were actually juggling the options. "Lobster Newburgh—boiled egg. Big decision."

"Not for somebody who doesn't happen to like lobster. Other seafood, yes—but not lobster."

"Steak, then. Or we could put it another way—staying home with Gran, Janet and the television, or going out for dinner."

"Getting dressed up and keeping company with you and Mindy…. I'd have to think about it." The trouble was, Lissa reflected, she *didn't* have to think about it. Kurt won that competition hands down.

But only because it would be fun to watch Mindy throwing out lures, she told herself. It certainly didn't have anything to do with spending the evening with Kurt.

"Don't forget that Ray's coming, too," Kurt reminded.

"Well, that fact certainly tips the scale in favor of going."

"Was that sarcasm I heard in your voice? I agree there's something freaky about that guy."

"Oh, you're just still holding it against him that he turned out not to be a woman."

"As if that would improve him. Go change your clothes—we need to get moving."

"Eager to see Mindy again?" Lissa said sweetly. She didn't wait for an answer.

Since there was only one good dress hanging in the guestroom closet, it didn't take her long to decide what to wear. When she came back into the living room Kurt was staring into the fire, glass in hand.

"Back already?" he said. "Maybe you're the one who's eager to see Ray."

She held her tongue until they were safely out of the house, but as she settled into the Jaguar Lissa said, "I want to make it clear that I only came because we need to brainstorm a new plan on approaching Hannah. She doesn't like the idea of an auction or a tag sale, or your friend in real estate. And arguing about it with her obviously isn't going to change anything—since you've already tried and she just walked out of the room."

"Then what do you recommend?"

"It's the idea of a sale that bothers her. She'll happily *give* things away, just not sell them."

"So maybe we just put a sign in front of the house that says *Free Stuff,* and let people in off the street to choose what they want?"

"And hire riot police to control the crowd? Do you want me to get in the backseat with Ray when we pick them up, so you can have Mindy up front with you?"

"I have an even better idea. You drive—"

"You're offering to let me get behind the wheel of your Jaguar? Pardon me a minute, I'm hyperventilating at the mere thought."

"Because then they'll take a cab home afterwards rather than risk another ride with you."

"You're funny," Lissa said. "Just for that I should take you up on it—and *you* can ride in back with Ray."

The address Mindy had given was two suburbs away, and rush hour was still going strong as they drove across the city. Kurt slid in and out of traffic with apparent ease, though Lissa closed her eyes every now and then, while he merged into a lane where she'd have sworn there wasn't room for a bicycle.

"What's the matter?" he asked finally. "Afraid I'm going to hit something?"

"Well, a nice little fender-bender would get us out of dinner," she pointed out.

"If this was my car, I'd consider it."

She frowned. "Whose is it?"

"A rental. I flew in from Boston."

"Boston? Do you have a store there?"

"Not yet. It's on the list for next year."

"You know, Kurt, I really don't understand why you don't want Hannah's house."

"For one thing, it's not in Seattle."

"But neither are you, most of the time—at least it doesn't sound as if you spend any time at home."

"Not a lot," he admitted.

"And that's my point—Minneapolis is much more centrally located, so you could have more time at home and still be able to get to all your stores in a hurry. The house is even reasonably close to the airport, and there must be a dozen airlines serving the Twin Cities. You could catch a flight to anywhere, anytime."

"Assuming I used airlines."

"You don't? I thought you said trying to fly off the garage roof with a couple of kites taught you a lesson."

"It did. I bought myself a corporate jet."

Of course he'd have a private plane. "Well, that's just one more thing we have in common," Lissa said dryly. "Neither of us collects frequent-flier miles."

He grinned at her. "You wouldn't know what to do with them, would you?"

She didn't bother to answer that. "Why do you live in Seattle, anyway? If your first store was in Denver, and you're such a fan of mountain-climbing—"

"I wanted to get out of Colorado. And Washington has mountains."

"Oh," she said. "Was it a girlfriend or a business deal that went bad?"

She thought for a second that he wasn't going to answer. "Neither," he said finally. "After four years of college I'd sort of forgotten how angry my parents were with each other. But as soon as I went home to Denver it all came back to me. I'd already started the first store, so I had to stick around for a while—but as soon as it was established enough that I could hire a manager I moved."

"They were getting a divorce?"

"No, they did that when I was three. The odd thing about those two is that they never moved on. Even after twenty years they were still so angry at each other that they couldn't talk about anything else."

"What were they fighting about? Custody of you?"

"Sort of. And money, of course. And new spouses—every one of them. And who'd broken whose favorite possession when they were still married. And where they should live."

"They argued about where to live *after* they were divorced?"

"Yeah. What was that address again?"

"I've got it here somewhere." Lissa dug into her coat pocket. Obviously the subject was closed, though her curiosity was far from satisfied. How did a couple *sort of* fight over custody of their son? And that bit about his parents' favorite possessions—did that explain why Kurt lived in a shoebox and didn't want to get attached to anything material?

She knew better than to pry; he'd told her as much as he was going to. He'd shared just a bit of what had made him the man he was.

And he'd left her wanting to know a whole lot more.

By the time they dropped off Mindy and Ray at Marian Meadows's house after dinner and dancing, it was threatening to snow again. The sky was low, the air felt heavy, and despite valiant efforts the streetlights seemed to make no dent in the gloom. Which made the weather pretty much a perfect metaphor for the entire evening, in Kurt's opinion.

He turned the Jaguar back into the street with a sigh of relief, and then wished he hadn't inhaled quite so deeply. The cloud of scent which had surrounded Mindy all evening seemed to have remained behind in the car. He'd no doubt have to air the vehicle out before he could return it to the rental agency.

Lissa, newly settled in the passenger seat beside

him, stretched, dug her hands into the pockets of her overcoat, and started whistling under her breath.

Whistling. Kurt couldn't believe his ears.

She broke off after a block or two and said, "Well, that wasn't bad. As dates go, I mean."

"It wasn't a date."

She looked over at him, brows arched. "Well, don't bite my head off about it. I think I was pretty tolerant, considering you left me no choice at all about going."

"What's that you're whistling?"

"I'm not whistling anything."

"You are. Either that or you're having a low-grade asthma attack."

"So what's the matter with whistling?"

"Nothing. I'm glad one of us had a good time."

"I did, as a matter of fact—thank you for asking. The steak was very good, and once Ray had made a clean breast of the whole plot he was quite a pleasant companion. I really enjoyed watching Mindy perform. I see sorority girls all the time at the student union, but this was the first chance I'd had to observe closely and see why they're so different from other people. It all seems to lie in the expectations."

Kurt growled, and she shut up. But, as he'd expected, the silence was too good to last. After a single minute of quiet, she started in again.

"You know, it was pretty funny, actually," she said. "I thought you were going to drop your fork when Ray finally spit out what he wanted. All that posturing and scheming they've been doing—everything you thought was intended to get Mindy and you together—and it turns out all Marian wanted was for you to give Ray a job."

"Are you really naive enough to think that was the whole plan, Lissa?"

"And are *you* really arrogant enough to think they're still after you? Or are you disappointed to find out how wrong you were?"

"I've been around this track before. No matter how many times you run the race, the scenery never varies."

"Well, that's poetic. Are you going to hire him?"

"Actually, I find it humorous that someone who wants to work in Human Resources has to pull strings to get a job."

"That's no answer."

"You're right, it wasn't. Why are you interested? Are you making sure he can afford to take you out in style before you encourage him?"

"No. Because if the tactic works, I might try it myself."

He swung the car into his grandmother's driveway. Most of the lights were off, but the bulb above the porte cochere was burning brightly. He parked the Jaguar directly under it.

"Hannah's left a night-light on for us," Lissa said. "Isn't that sweet? She probably thought it would be the wee hours before we got in."

"Instead, it only feels like we've been gone for three days. Are you going to get out of the car and come in, or just sit there getting high on Mindy's perfume the rest of the night?"

Lissa didn't move. "I'm waiting for you to come around and open my door," she said with dignity.

"I'm not the chauffeur—or the parking valet."

"You did it for Mindy," she reminded him. "It's that expectation thing, I suspect. She sat still, and you finally remembered your manners."

"I was anxious to get rid of her. You, on the other hand—"

"You're not anxious to get rid of me?" she asked brightly.

"The situation's completely reversed. If you sit out here I won't have to deal with you at all. Good night."

But, though his door was already open, he didn't get out of the car. Something—he couldn't put his finger on what it was—seemed to be pressing him back into his seat, keeping him there.

You're not anxious to get rid of me? Of course he was. And yet....

Because if the tactic works, I might try it myself....

The very idea of Lissa trying to seduce him into hiring her made his head swim. Which was a whole lot more than he could say for Mindy's methods. Maybe he'd just play along for a while and see what happened.

He leaned back against the headrest and half

turned to face her. "You're sure you're waiting for me to open your door? You wouldn't—just possibly—be waiting for something else, would you?"

"Like what?" An instant later he saw comprehension dawn in her eyes, and he reached across her and intercepted her hand just as she touched the door handle. "Kurt, if you think I'm sitting here waiting to be kissed—"

"You kissed Ray good night."

"That was different." She blinked. "I mean…."

It was, Kurt thought, the funniest thing any of them had said all evening. "Different from how I'm going to kiss you? You can take that to the bank."

"It was just a peck on the cheek. It wasn't even intended to be a kiss. There was an audience, for heaven's sake, and—"

"And now there isn't," he murmured. "And you might think about how I'm doing you a favor at the moment by shutting you up so you can't dig yourself in any deeper." His fingers were still encircling her wrist, and he drew her slowly closer to him across the car.

She could protest all she wanted, he thought, but the truth was in her eyes. Even in the dim interior of the car he could see uncertainty mixed with desire in the deep brown pools. And the truth was in her body, in the way she went limp in his arms, as if she'd lost control of every muscle, every nerve. Everything but her mouth, which more than made up for the rest.

Just as it had that first time, so many years ago. The very first time he'd kissed her, when he'd realized that the most explosive substance on earth wasn't plutonium, but Lissa Morgan's innocence.

That was different, she'd said. Yes, it sure as hell was. If she'd made any move to kiss Ray like this….

Anxious to get rid of her? Not on her life. Not just yet, at any rate.

It was the wind whipping through his opened car door which finally brought him back to reality. "Let's go inside," he said. Obediently, as if half-asleep, Lissa reached for the passenger door handle again. But Kurt didn't let go—instead, he gently tugged until she slid across the seat and out his door.

He didn't have a plan, and he hadn't thought any further than getting inside where it was warm—or at least he hadn't given the matter any conscious thought. But the instant the door opened and he saw the pool of dim light in the living room he realized that what he really wanted to do was absolutely impossible. He could hardly hustle Lissa up the stairs and into his room—into his bed—when his grandmother was sitting up waiting for them.

Hotel, he thought vaguely. Why hadn't he insisted on staying in a hotel?

"You're home already?" Hannah called, and Kurt pushed the door shut and crossed the hall.

His grandmother was settled on the couch with a pot of hot chocolate on the table beside her, a magazine open on her lap, and Lissa's quilt spread over her knees.

"I hope you don't mind me using your quilt, dear," she said. "It was getting chilly, with the fire dying down."

"Of course I don't mind." Lissa's voice had a breathy catch and she looked dazed, Kurt thought. In fact, she looked as if she'd been thoroughly kissed.

He tried to stay between her and Hannah, hoping Gran wouldn't get a good enough view to figure out what had happened.

"It's actually sort of Kurt's quilt, though."

Gran looked intrigued. "Really?"

"Just a joke, Gran," he said hastily, before she jumped to the conclusion that he'd changed his mind about all the heirloom junk she wanted to give him.

"I'm going on up to bed," Lissa said. "It'll be a busy day again tomorrow." She managed a smile. "Since you've had a rest, Hannah, I imagine you'll be a slave driver in the morning." She stumbled a bit as she left the room.

"Isn't she a lovely girl?" Gran murmured.

Every warning buzzer Kurt had ever heard seemed to be chiming in unison in his head. What was his grandmother up to now? Maybe it *wasn't* Mindy she'd been aiming at him...?

He shrugged and made sure that not even a hopeful grandmother could read enthusiasm into his voice. "I suppose so."

"Oh, I'd say there's no doubt at all about it. And they make such a cute couple, don't they? Ray and Lissa, I mean."

"Yeah." *Wait a minute. What's she talking about?* "Gran, did you say *Ray and Lissa*?"

"Yes, dear. What's wrong? Surely you didn't think I was trying to pair her up with *you*? Heavens, Kurt—I *like* Lissa too much to see her be wasted." She picked up her mug and sipped. "I only stayed up to apologize, you know—I'm sorry I was a bit sharp with you earlier, about your friend in real estate. Would you like some hot chocolate? There's more here in the pot. Do sit down, Kurt, and let's have a heart-to-heart chat—about everything."

CHAPTER EIGHT

LISSA LAY AWAKE for a long time, thinking about what had happened in the car. Why must she be such a—such a *sponge* about being kissed? Add water to a sponge and you could mold it into any shape you liked. Add a simple kiss to Lissa Morgan and she, too, went all pliable and soppy....

Of course, she admitted, that analogy wasn't quite true, because it hadn't exactly been a simple kiss. If a simple kiss was like a jazz piece, then this embrace—with its multiple undertones and nuances—had been a full-fledged symphony.

And it wasn't just any kiss which could affect her that way, either. She'd been kissed her fair share of times, and never with anyone else had she reacted the way she did when Kurt Callahan touched her.

Of course, that didn't mean there was anything incredible going on here. No once-in-a-lifetime fireworks exploding. All it meant was that Kurt was far more experienced than the usual guys who'd kissed her goodnight at the door. And it wasn't exactly something to be proud of that she reacted like clockwork to a professional. Particularly when she knew from firsthand experience what an experienced charmer he was.

Maybe it was the unexpectedness that really got her, she speculated. Every time he'd kissed her, she'd had only an instant's warning, barely time to brace herself and certainly not enough to mentally prepare. So what if next time she didn't wait around for him to get the idea? What if she seized every opportunity to kiss *him,* rather than let him kiss her? Then she'd be the one in control. She'd be ready. And before long she'd be bored out of her skull and he wouldn't affect her at all anymore…

Dreamer, whispered a little voice in the back of her brain. *You just want an excuse to kiss him again.*

She punched her pillow into shape and thought about what little he'd said about his parents and Denver. No wonder the man was skittish about women, about commitment, about sentimental attachment to material goods.

And no wonder her resistance had been softened. Who wouldn't be sympathetic after a tale like that? Even though the details were few and the emotions were mostly ones she'd imagined for herself?

She wondered what Kurt and Hannah were talking about down in the living room, and why it seemed to be taking so long. She didn't even realize she was listening for footsteps on the stairs until she heard them come up. Hannah's steps were slow and careful, as if she were tired or discouraged. Then, quite a bit later, Lissa heard Kurt—though he was obviously trying to be quiet. Was it her imagination, or did he pause outside her door before going on upstairs to his own room?

Surely not. Kissing her was one thing, but coming to her room…. Unless there was something he needed to tell her, to warn her about. Perhaps something concerning his conversation with Hannah.

How much did Hannah know—or suspect?

Her comment about expecting Hannah to be a slave driver in the morning, after her evening's rest, had been nothing more than a casual phrase, but Lissa had barely left her room before she was starting to feel that she'd had a psychic moment.

A muffled thump drew her attention to the dressing room right next to Hannah's bedroom. Her "extra wardrobe," Hannah had called it, and Lissa had taken one look through the door at a couple of bulging closets and decided to postpone the job as long as she could.

Now, she opened the door and paused in horrified surprise at the sight of Hannah, standing on a chair, taking boxes off the top shelf of a closet. One of them had escaped her and bounced on the carpet.

She was eighty, and the woman was standing on

a chair cleaning out shelves. It was a wonder she hadn't fallen off.

"Good heavens, Hannah," she said. "How did you get up there?"

"I climbed on the hassock and then onto the chair. I thought I'd get an early start, and I didn't want to bother you since you were out late last night."

Lissa, feeling guilty, stooped to pick up the hatbox Hannah had dropped, and eyed the row of similar boxes which marched across the top of the dresser. The woman had obviously been at work for quite a while. "What's got you so fired up today?"

"I had a chat with Kurt last night."

Lissa wondered if that was good news or bad. If Kurt had told his grandmother he wanted to use her china for target practice….

Hannah pulled another box from the closet shelf and opened it. "Oh, this was one of my favorites— back in the days when women wore hats every-where. Maybe I should bring them back into style."

Lissa blinked at the bright-eyed bird—it looked real—perched atop the forest-green velvet. "Well, I wouldn't suggest starting with that one, or all the animal lovers will be on your case. Of course you could wear it with the mink and give them a two-for-one thrill." She took the box and added it to the row on the dresser.

Hannah didn't seem to share the joke. "There's a suit in here—the hat matches it. The same shade of green, but it's wool trimmed in velvet." She bent over, wobbling a little, so she could flip through the dress bags which hung under the shelf, peeking at each hanger.

Lissa's throat tightened. "Hannah," she said firmly. "You get down this minute and let me look for it."

"I wonder who might be able to use these things?" Hannah mused. Obediently, she took Lissa's hand and got down from the chair to the hassock, and then to the floor, groaning a little. Lissa felt the pressure in her chest ease a bit with Hannah safely back on firm ground.

"Why don't you go downstairs for a rest and a cup of coffee? I'll think about who would want them," Lissa suggested. "Oh, this must be the one you were looking for." She pulled out an organdy dress bag and opened it. "This is gorgeous."

The cut of the suit was severe and so old-fashioned that it was now back in style. Lissa could almost covet it herself. She laid the bag across the bed and set the matching hat on top of it. "I bet the drama department at the university would like having authentic period costumes."

"Oh, goodness." Hannah sighed. "Hearing my wardrobe referred to as *authentic period costumes* is a bit of a jolt."

"Sorry."

"It's all right, dear. It's true, after all. I'll bring

you a cup of coffee—or would you like to have breakfast before you start sorting?"

"I'm not hungry. But I'd love coffee." Lissa climbed up on the chair and took out the next hatbox in the row.

She was admiring a confection of ivory silk and net, with iridescent beads scattered over it to catch the light, when she heard a footstep behind her. "What did you do with all these clothes, Hannah?"

It was Kurt who answered. "She wore them, I presume."

Lissa spun around, forgetting she was standing on a chair, and only kept her balance by dropping the hat and bracing both hands on the molding atop the closet door. She must look as if she were hanging by her fingernails, she thought irritably. Very carefully she shifted her grip and regained her balance. "I thought you'd already left."

"I slept in this morning." He retrieved the hat and handed it back to her.

"Thanks. Still recuperating from the talking-to you got from Hannah, perhaps?"

"That would take a while." His voice was dry.

The almost-devious answer was all the confirmation Lissa needed—it was obvious to her, if she'd needed confirmation, that the subject had been Lissa herself. "I'll accept your apology now, for causing all this trouble."

His eyebrows tilted upward. "If you're expecting

me to say I'm sorry for kissing you last night, get over it. You were much too cooperative to deserve an apology."

Lissa bit her lip. She could hardly deny that. *You're nothing but a sponge,* she accused herself. "Then I'll accept with gratitude your offer to explain to your grandmother that there's nothing going on between us."

"With *gratitude,* yet? That's too bad. Because I'm going to do nothing of the sort."

"But there isn't, Kurt. A few kisses don't mean anything." She didn't look directly at him. She wasn't sure she wanted to see the expression on his face. Would it be relief to find that she agreed with him? Satisfaction, perhaps, that she hadn't misinterpreted his intentions?

He moved the forest-green suit and sat down on the corner of the bed. "What do you think our talk last night was about, anyway?"

"Well…." There was no easy way to put it. "Me. Or I should say, you and me? Right?"

He grinned. "Now who's being arrogant?"

"But what else could it be? She talked to you last night, and today she's suddenly gung-ho to get this room cleaned out. I thought it must be because she's suspicious of what's going on, and she wants to hurry things along and get me out of here."

"I thought," Kurt said meditatively, "you said there was nothing going on."

"But if she thinks there is…."

"She doesn't."

Lissa frowned. How could Hannah not be suspicious, considering the way Lissa had come staggering in last night after that assault on her senses had robbed her of all fine motor control? "I suppose as a cover story you told her I'd had too much to drink?"

"I didn't tell her a thing—because she didn't ask. In fact, I think you're just feeling guilty, Lissa—and considering that you say yourself there's nothing to feel guilty about, I find that very interesting."

She could feel herself turning slightly pink.

"Relax. Gran thinks you and Ray make a cute couple."

Lissa blinked in surprise. "Okay. Well, I suppose that makes things easier."

"One would think so. Of course that's not what she wanted to talk to me about either. But I don't suppose it'll come as any surprise to you that she's giving you the house."

Lissa's foot slid off the chair cushion, and this time she *was* literally hanging from the top of the closet door.

Kurt stepped forward, slid an arm around her waist, and lifted her down.

"Thanks." She was feeling shaky. "You know, maybe I should have something to eat. I'm so out of it that I'd have sworn you said—"

"I did say it. She's planning to give you the house. This house."

Blood was pounding in Lissa's ears. "That's impossible. She hasn't said a word to me about it."

"Since when did Gran consult anybody—unless it was convenient for her to blame somebody else for the idea?"

He had a point there. As her breathing finally steadied, Lissa's mind finally started to work right again. "Oh, now I understand. Of course she wouldn't tell me about it. She told you she was going to give me the house because she has no intention of actually doing it."

Kurt shook his head as if it hurt. "Run that one by me again."

"It was a shock tactic. She tells you that you're not getting the house, the shock makes you realize that you'd be heartbroken to lose it, so you argue with her about how she shouldn't give it to me, and *voilà!* She allows herself to be persuaded that it should stay in the family and then everybody's happy—including Lissa, who never knew what she missed out on."

"That's not what happened."

"You didn't have a sudden revelation that you want it?"

"Nope. I think it's an idiotic idea, but not because I had an attack of envy. The way is clear for you."

"But I don't want it! I don't know what on earth made her think I might."

"You haven't dropped any little hints about how wonderful the place is?"

"Well…only to make her think about whether she really wants to leave it."

"No chats about how if I would only stop to think I'd change my mind, because it's such a wonderful house and a family treasure? No discussions of how a central location would be better for my business?"

"Not to her. I swear, Kurt, I only told you that on the spur of the moment last night. What would I do with this house, anyway? It's way too big for her and Janet, so why she'd even consider giving it to me…. I could live in the linen closet and never touch the other rooms."

"Well, there you have it." Kurt's voice was dry. "You'd have plenty of room, now that the sheets and towels are all gone, and she could leave all her stuff here and come visit it whenever she liked."

"You think I conned her," Lissa said quietly. "Don't you?"

"No," Kurt said finally. "Not exactly." He pushed himself up off the bed and left the room.

A couple of minutes later Hannah came back, with two big mugs of coffee. "Here you go, Lissa. Maybe we should talk to the people in the drama department before we drag all this stuff out of the closets."

Lissa's jaw dropped. Now that she'd started the job, Hannah was suddenly ready to quit? What could have changed the woman's mind? Had Kurt run into her on the stairs and said something?

"We should look everything over and make a list anyway. I think they'd be more interested if there was some sort of inventory they could look at before deciding." Lissa took a long pull from her coffee and felt warmth creep through her veins.

She still couldn't believe what Kurt had told her. He must have been mistaken. She would have to think of a way to gently broach the subject with Hannah. She could hardly just say, *Is it true you want to give me your house?* Because if that wasn't what Hannah had said…well, the uproar would be incredible.

"I can take care of the inventory," Lissa went on, "as long as you'll pop in once in a while to identify things. I'm afraid I wouldn't know a cloche from a cloak without help."

"No, I'll just sit here and write it all down as you go. Are you sure you don't want a break, though?"

Lissa shook her head, finished clearing the shelf, and looked with interest at the set of cabinets which had been built in above the closet doors to take advantage of the enormous height of the ceilings. How was she supposed to get to those? The items in those cupboards—and she had no doubt the space was full—would probably be even older and more interesting than what was in the closet.

She decided to think about it later, and climbed down off the chair.

"Did you have fun on your date last night?" Hannah asked. She had dug a box of stationery out of a desk drawer and was trying pens, tossing one after another aside before finding one which worked. "Goodness, I didn't realize it had been so long since this room was used."

Kurt pushed the door wide and brought in a shiny new aluminum ladder. "Stop climbing on chairs. You can't come to the party at the store on Friday if you're in the hospital with a broken hip, Gran."

"A Christmas party?" Hannah asked brightly.

"As soon as the doors close on Christmas Eve."

"I love Christmas parties," Hannah said. "And I bet Lissa does, too. As long as you promise to get us home in time to be tucked in before Santa Claus comes."

Kurt left for the store before Lissa could catch him alone, and a couple of hours later the closet was empty. The bed was piled with dresses and suits, shoes and handbags, and Lissa was tugging the ladder into position for an assault on the top cabinets.

Hannah sighed. It was a long, heavy, tired sigh, and to Lissa it seemed to echo through the room.

"Kurt thinks the same thing you do." Hannah didn't look up from her list. "That I should just walk away from all this and have a sale."

"He doesn't want to see you exhaust yourself."

Hannah didn't answer.

Lissa sat down on the bed, where she could

watch Hannah's profile as she wrote. "Actually, that's where Kurt and I disagree," Lissa said. "I don't think you should hire an auctioneer."

Hannah raised her eyebrows. "Indeed?"

"Maybe the university would like to have the house. Perhaps they could turn it into a museum of costume and design."

Hannah turned the sheet of stationery over and began a new column. "I'm sure Kurt told you that I've decided what to do with the house, Lissa. I'm going to give it to you."

Until that moment Lissa had kept telling herself that Kurt had been mistaken, that he must have heard his grandmother wrong.

"But *why?*" Her voice sounded like a screech. "Hannah, what are you *thinking?*"

Hannah sounded perfectly calm. "I want you to have it because I like you, and because you like my house."

"But what on earth would I do with it?"

"Live in it, I hope."

"Hannah, I couldn't possibly afford…." Lissa's voice failed, and she had to start over. "The electric bill alone must be staggering. To say nothing of how I'd manage the upkeep, along with going to school. And how I'd even *get* to school—"

"Because the house is too far from campus for easy commuting?" Hannah asked calmly. "I know that. It's exactly why the university wouldn't possibly want to make it into a museum, either. It was a good try, though, Lissa. Was that Kurt's idea, or yours?"

"Mine," Lissa muttered. She eyed Hannah suspiciously. "You're not serious, of course. You only told me you want to give me the house so I'd have to admit the museum idea wasn't a very good one—right?"

"Oh, no. I'm quite serious. I figure you can rent the house out until you're finished with school, and that will help with your tuition and living expenses. Then, when you have a job and an adequate income, you'll be able to afford to live here yourself."

Lissa put her head in her hands. "That's the most—"

"Careful, my dear. I'm only an old lady, and everyone keeps insisting I'm in fragile health. I'm sure you don't want to upset me."

Upset her? At the moment the woman bore an uncanny resemblance to an Abrams tank, Lissa thought—capable of running straight over any opposition.

"And then you can remodel it however you like," Hannah went on comfortably.

Lissa grabbed for the straw. "You wouldn't mind if I changed things?"

"Oh, I'm not silly enough to think the house is perfect just as it is. It could be made much more comfortable."

"But *that's* the answer, then. You stay right here. Instead of investing in a retirement community, put the money into making the house easier to handle for you and Janet. And leave everything else alone. You don't need the room, so you can stop cleaning closets and dragging boxes out from under beds—"

"I'd still have all the headaches of owning a house. And someday when I'm gone, Kurt would still hire an auctioneer to come in and sell everything."

Lissa bit her lip. She didn't think it would be much comfort to remind the woman that after she was dead she wouldn't much care what happened to her hats, her china, her Christmas ornaments….

"He means well," Lissa said finally. "He just doesn't realize that things can be so important. But that doesn't mean he never will appreciate sentiment."

Hannah smiled then. "And if I live to be two hundred I might yet see it. Do you want to call the people at the drama department about all these clothes, or shall I?"

The caterers had set up the buffet tables even before the mall doors were locked, and within minutes of closing time on Christmas Eve the food was arranged and the staff had begun to gather in the large center atrium of the store. Kurt could hear the rumble of conversation as he made a last-minute check of total sales figures in all the stores.

"How's it look, boss?" the store manager asked. "How are we doing in comparison?"

"Pretty well. The bonus checks came in, didn't they?"

The manager patted his pocket. "I thought I'd start with that, as soon as everybody's here." He grinned. "Nothing like some unexpected money to loosen up a party. Do you want to do the honors?"

Kurt shook his head. "That's your job. I'm only here by accident." He signed off the network and left the computer to idle.

"Fine with me—I'm happy to be the bearer of good news. I saw your grandmother come in, by the way. She and a gorgeous girl are waiting for you down by the buffet. The girl asked where you were."

Gorgeous girl. Lissa, of course. There was no reason for the manager's comment to send his blood pressure up; any man with eyes could see that though Lissa might not be conventionally beautiful, she was stunning in all the ways that mattered.

He saw them from the top of the escalator. Hannah with her coat slung carelessly around her shoulders, Lissa wearing a dark green suit that hugged her figure and made her look even more like an undernourished waif.

He joined them near the buffet table. Lissa was holding a plate, he saw. It was decorated with a chunk of broccoli, a bit of cauliflower, a radish, and a celery stick. He took it away from her. "No dieting allowed on the premises tonight. Have a pile of shrimp instead."

"Maybe later." Her gaze followed his grand-mother a few steps toward the table, and she lowered her voice. "I need to talk to you. Alone."

Kurt didn't miss a beat. "Your climbing gear came in. Want to come take a look?"

Lissa rolled her eyes, but she grabbed the cue. "Of course. We'll be back in a minute, Hannah."

His grandmother waved a casual hand, seem-ingly too intent on inspecting the ice sculpture cen-terpiece to notice whether they were present or not.

As they walked away, Lissa muttered, "You couldn't think of a better cover than suggesting I'm going to be climbing that stupid wall?"

"Hey, it worked. That's a nice suit, by the way. When did you and Gran fit in time to shop?"

"We didn't. This came straight out of Hannah's closet and it's older than I am. But we are making significant dents."

"Dents? And that would explain why I've been climbing over piles to get in and out of the house?"

"At least it's not the same pile," Lissa defended. "In the last two days I've been back to the homeless shelter, to the library with books to donate, to a support group for single moms to drop off yarn and knitting needles to make baby booties, and to a senior citizens' center where they sew stuffed animals from old fabric for the Red Cross to hand out at fires. Hannah's dressing room is still a wreck, but that's because the drama department at the university is closed down along with everything else this week, so we can't get rid of the vintage clothes." She flicked a hand across her skirt.

"So you're wearing the stuff instead? Have you decided to accept Gran's gift?"

"The house? Do I look like I'm nuts? I don't need an ulcer on top of everything else."

"Then you understand how I feel about it."

"But what are we going to do, Kurt?" She paused for a deep breath and said thoughtfully, "You know, sometimes I get the impression that she'd really like to stay. I've been talking to her about remodeling, to make the house easier to live in, and if it wasn't for the work and mess and confusion that's involved I think she'd love your ideas."

"Wait a minute. *My* ideas?"

"Yes—that's why I needed to talk to you. To fill you in so you don't blow it if she happens to mention remodeling."

"Thoughtful of you. What great ideas have I had?"

"The main one involves turning the linen closet into a master bath and laundry room combination."

"Why on earth would I want to do that?"

"Because most laundry originates in the bedrooms. It's handier not to have to carry it all the way downstairs and then back up again. And the extra bath will be very useful when there are children."

"Hold everything right there. *Kids?* What are you telling her?"

"Just that you're still a young man, and eventually you'll settle down and—"

"You told Hannah *I* want the house? After all the fuss and frustration I've had to convince her otherwise?"

Lissa looked so innocent that he was tempted to wring her skinny little neck before she could zing him with any other surprises. Though he supposed it would be more sensible to wait till she'd spilled all the current ones first—just in case.

"Not exactly," she said carefully. "I may—possibly—have hinted that you're actually more fond of the place than you're letting on."

Which meant, of course, that she'd actually come straight out and said it. "Why?"

"Why am I sure that down deep you want it? Because it offended you so much when she tried to give it to me. And don't pretend it didn't, because I won't believe you. You were seething when you told me. Maybe you're planning for it to be your summer retreat? It's not like that would be anything new. And then eventually—"

"You've been telling her I want her to remodel the place and live in it till I'm ready to take it over? And that would be when? When I retire in forty years, maybe?"

"Well, yes. Sort of. Only I don't think she's going for it," Lissa admitted. "All the dust and noise of remodeling puts her right off the idea. So I was thinking, Kurt—if you were to send her and Janet on a round-the-world cruise…"

"And rebuild her house while she's gone? What if she comes home and announces that she still wants to move into the retirement home?"

She sighed. "Then I guess you'd have a very updated Dutch colonial."

"Or *you* would. She sounds pretty determined that you're going to end up with it."

"Maybe if I tell her I plan to turn the porte cochere into a party room, with a hot tub to seat eight, she'll change her mind about me being the right person to take care of her house." She looked over his shoulder. "Oops."

"What? Gran's on her way to find us?"

"Not quite."

Kurt turned around to see Mindy, simpering her way down the aisle toward them, a wide fake smile plastered on her face.

"Hello," she said. "This is odd, finding you two here. Hannah told me you'd be in the climbing department."

"We're just on our way back," Kurt said smoothly. "What brings you to the party?"

"Oh, Ray invited me. He said all the employees were told they could bring a guest."

Lissa's eyebrows had climbed. "Ray? You didn't tell me you'd hired him, Kurt."

And when, he wondered irritably, would he have

had the opportunity? Every time he'd seen her in the last few days she'd had her head in a cabinet or her hands full of boxes and bags. "Not all the new sales-people we hired when the store opened have worked out. That happens with any new store when there's an entirely new crew of workers."

"Nobody here is experienced?" She sounded disbelieving.

She's doing her accountant impression again. "The manager has been with me for years, and a few of the assistants."

"So that's what you've been doing all week—working as an ordinary sales clerk?"

"Among other things. It keeps me in touch with the customers."

"I'd imagine it does."

Mindy, obviously annoyed at being left out of the exchange, said, "So you've decided to start climbing after all, Lissa. I wonder what could possibly have made you change your mind about that."

"Isn't it obvious?" Lissa said sweetly. "It's my utter fascination with everything about Kurt. I'm sure you understand the feeling…."

Kurt could have cheerfully knocked their heads together. "I'm going after some food," he announced. "The boxing ring's over that way, if you two want to suit up and go at it."

Boxing ring, Lissa thought. As if she'd fight over him—though she had no doubts that Mindy would.

Much as she'd enjoyed jabbing Kurt about his ego, she had to admit that Mindy's intentions were pretty obvious.

Mindy laughed, a mincing little tinkle that—to Lissa, at least—didn't sound at all amused. "How very tacky it would be of us to squabble in public— as if you're a toy we both want." She slid a hand through the curve of Kurt's elbow, and the two of them moved off toward the rising noise from the party.

Lissa followed along in their wake, quite happy to be ignored for the moment. What on earth had inspired her to descend to Mindy's level, anyway?

The party was in full swing. The tables of food already looked ravaged, the store's music system had been turned up, and a few employees were dancing in the atrium. Kurt and Mindy were immediately swallowed up in the crowd, but Lissa dawdled behind.

She wasn't unnoticed, however, for as she paused on the edge of the party Ray came up beside her, his plate loaded with snacks. "Hi, Lissa."

"This is a surprise, Ray. Kurt tells me you're working here now." She took a closer look. She'd gotten the distinct impression from Kurt just a few minutes ago that Ray was just one more salesclerk. Yet, in a sea of Maximum Sports' standard blue employees' pullovers, here was Ray, dressed as neatly as any vice-president in a white shirt and a necktie any CEO would be proud of. "What are you doing?" The question was idle; Lissa was watching Mindy, who hadn't loosened her hold on Kurt's arm, playing hostess.

"Not the job I wanted, of course." Ray sounded defensive. "And not anywhere near what I'm qualified for. But he was short-handed, so I'm happy to help out."

Sales, Lissa thought. Well, if Kurt was working the floor himself, it wasn't too much to ask Ray to do the same. "Lots of us don't get the jobs we want, Ray."

"You've got a pretty sweet deal right now," he said. "Hey, with all your connections, have you heard anything about Kurt moving the company headquarters here?"

That's a big oops, Lissa thought. *I just hope Kurt doesn't hear that one.*

It wasn't hard to figure out where the story had come from, of course. Lissa had hinted to Hannah that Kurt would like to keep the house in the family, and from there it would have been only a small step for Hannah to convince herself that he actually wanted to live in it. Which, of course, meant that he would want to work nearby. And if she'd breathed a word of that line of thought to her friend Marian….

"Where'd you hear that?" she asked casually.

"Around." Obviously he wasn't going to confide in her.

"From Marian?"

He looked genuinely surprised. "Does she know?"

Lissa could have sworn at herself for the slip-up. "I doubt there's anything to know. If there was something to it Hannah would probably have told Marian—that's all I meant."

"Yeah, I suppose." Ray didn't sound satisfied. "I hear he's been talking to real-estate people."

She was relieved to be able to quash part of the story. "Oh, that's because of Hannah's house. Nothing to do with the business. Put it out of your mind."

"Well, you see, I was hoping that if he *did* move the headquarters there would be a spot in the personnel office for me."

Lissa smiled at him. "Good luck. But I don't have any influence, I'm afraid."

The music died and the store manager stepped forward. "Is everybody having a good time? Don't worry, I'm not announcing work schedules for next week, and I'll let you get back to partying in a minute. In the meantime, though, Santa made an early stop—assisted by our boss—" he paused to let the applause die down "—and he asked me to distribute a few small gifts." He pulled a pile of envelopes from the inside pocket of his jacket. "I'm going to call names."

Ray was intent on listening, but because there was no reason for Lissa to pay attention she tuned out and wandered toward a display of windchimes. They were so perfectly balanced that even the movement of people in the atrium caused them to murmur. She closed her eyes and listened to the soft music of the chimes, to the voice droning names, and the happy chatter of those who had already opened their envelopes.

"Let's all thank Kurt," the manager suggested, and this time the applause seemed to take forever to die down. "Now, just one more thing. I'd like to introduce someone else who has a few words to say—someone who just this week received a donation from our boss: a full gym setup for the men of the Mission Shelter downtown."

That got Lissa's attention. The Mission Shelter was where he'd gone with her just last Sunday, to deliver a load of sheets, towels and soap.

It was very interesting, she thought, that when she'd told him just a few minutes ago about going back to the shelter with another donation he hadn't mentioned his own gift. Interesting—and also very much like Kurt, she thought, to try to avoid getting the credit. He hadn't bragged about hiring Ray, either. And Hannah had told her he'd even tried to duck out of that banquet in his honor at the university.

Well, she was glad he hadn't managed to avoid that evening's festivities, or she would never have met him again. She would never have come to love him....

The realization was so smooth, so natural, that for a moment Lissa didn't even realize what she was thinking. Then the fact hit her as hard as if the climbing wall had suddenly crumbled on top of her.

For the last six years he'd always been at the back of her mind. He'd been her first lover, and there was *no* forgetting that. But all this time, while she'd thought she'd been nursing her irritation at him, and the hurt and humiliation of the past, she'd been fooling herself. She'd been getting more deeply involved with each conversation, each smile—each kiss. And as she had gotten to know the real man, she had fallen in love with him.

There's nothing going on between us, she'd said. Which was true enough.

The problem was, she didn't want it to be true—because she wanted Kurt to care as much about her as she cared about him.

CHAPTER NINE

LISSA WAS HORRIFIED by the sudden realization. How was it possible that she'd fallen in love with a guy who had actually made a bet on whether he could turn a tutoring session into making love? A guy who had not only made the bet but carried it through, won it, and bragged about it?

I didn't tell them, he'd said a few days ago, and he'd sounded perfectly sincere. Was it possible she'd been mistaken? Had he really been the arrogant and self-centered jerk she'd convinced herself he was back then?

Or was he the young man whose bitter, angry parents had fought over him and left him scarred?

In any case, he wasn't like that now. He'd proved it, because she had given him plenty of opportunities to take advantage of her again in the last few days and he hadn't done it.

Lissa didn't think that his failure to act was entirely due to respect for his grandmother, or even the fact that for the moment he was living under Hannah's roof—some of those occasions hadn't involved Hannah at all. In Lissa's room at the boarding house, where he'd kissed her and she'd melted into him, it hadn't been respect for his grandmother's feelings which had stopped him—any more than it had stopped Lissa herself. In his car, after that ill-conceived dinner date, the idea that Hannah might be waiting up for them had barely entered the equation. Then there was the apartment he'd offered to rent for Lissa—and the fact that he hadn't suggested it be a love nest for the two of them...

No, he hadn't take advantage of her—despite the many opportunities he'd had.

The many opportunities you created, Lissa admitted. Though just an hour ago she'd have let her toenails be pulled out rather than confess it even to herself, now she couldn't dodge the knowledge any longer. She hadn't exactly tried to avoid his kiss at the boarding house that day. And, no matter how she explained it, the fact was that Lissa herself had managed to arrange that dinner date and opened up the opportunity for a good night kiss.

But in every case Kurt had acted like an almost-perfect gentleman. Which, she had to admit, was a very lowering thought—for if it wasn't simple respect for his grandmother which had kept him from acting on the invitations Lissa had offered him, then what had stopped him?

Was he afraid that Lissa would misinterpret his intentions? Or was she fooling herself to think that the craving he'd felt on those occasions was as overwhelming as what she had experienced?

She didn't believe she could be mistaken altogether—there was no question in her mind that he had felt desire, for if he hadn't why would he have kissed her a second time, and a third? But maybe for him it hadn't been the same mind-blowing sort of hunger that had threatened to knock all common sense out of her head. Perhaps for Kurt it had just been ordinary lust—and not important enough to throw him off balance or make him forget simple caution.

Lissa had fallen in love—but it seemed that to Kurt she'd been nothing more than an interesting novelty, something to entertain himself with for a few days, but certainly nothing important enough to make him risk offending his grandmother.

She'd fallen straight into the same trap she had as an inexperienced coed—letting herself believe that the popular guy, the most handsome in the class, could be seriously interested in her. Only this time there hadn't been a bunch of his friends in the wings to make it clear how she'd been duped, so instead of quickly realizing her mistake—and running while there was still time—she'd fallen farther and faster than before. Because he was so different now she'd fallen even harder. And now there was no turning back.

She remembered how sure she'd been, after the foursome's dinner date, that Kurt had paused beside her bedroom door before he went on upstairs to his own. She remembered feeling left out and lonely that night, wanting him and hoping he wanted her—though at the time she hadn't begun to recognize what she was experiencing.

Had his feelings been entirely created in her imagination? Had she taken a few sparse, careless kisses and dreamed them into a passionate affair?

Or perhaps the entire situation was even worse than that. It would be bad enough if she had imagined that Kurt felt the same desire, the same longing that she did. But if he'd caught a hint of what she was thinking…that would certainly account for why he'd kept himself so busy all week.

Lissa had told herself for days that she was glad he was staying away from the house so much, that his absence made her life a great deal easier. Only now, after facing the greater truth, could she admit the reality—she had missed him almost beyond bearing.

She'd awakened every morning eager to see him, and she'd been disappointed to find that he was already gone for the day. Every precious minute that she had actually spent in his company—always, it seemed, with Hannah there, or Janet—

she'd been jealous, because she'd wanted to have him all to herself.

No wonder just half an hour ago, when Mindy had chased them down, interrupted their conversation, and started to flirt with Kurt, Lissa had reacted like a cat whose tail had been stepped on.

It's my utter fascination with everything about Kurt, she'd told Mindy. She'd intended the comment as sarcasm, but it was far from that. It was simple truth. She *was* utterly fascinated with everything about the man.

It was too late to erase the fact, to back out of loving him. And there was not a thing she could do to make him return her feelings. She'd done this to herself—and now she was stuck with the results.

Though it felt to Lissa as if a month or two had passed while she was standing at the fringes of the party and sorting out what had happened to her, in fact only a few minutes had gone by. When she pulled herself back to the atrium at the center of Maximum Sports, the windchimes were still murmuring softly and the director of the Mission Shelter was still giving thanks for the generous gift.

Kurt, she noticed, was looking around as if he wished he were anywhere else.

Lissa couldn't quite keep herself from smiling at the way he was shifting from one foot to the other, looking in turn at the marble floor and the glass dome of the atrium. Definitely he wasn't the same guy he'd been in calculus class, she thought. Then he'd been nothing short of arrogant, while now he exuded a self-confidence that was based in fact rather than attitude. He'd gone out into the world and made it his.

The rush of warmth which surged through her at the thought took her by surprise, almost rocking her off her feet. Was this what love felt like? Not a flood of passion—though she didn't doubt that it lurked not far under the surface—but an incredible wave of tenderness. Fondness. Affection. Sheer liking.

It wasn't at all what she would have expected.

The shelter director stopped talking, and there was a burst of applause. Then Lissa heard Kurt's voice. It seemed to her to ring out above the noise of the crowd, even though his tone was actually low and almost intimate. How was it she could hear him so clearly? Had she simply tuned her hearing so that she wouldn't miss anything he said?

He was talking to Mindy, and it was very clear to Lissa what the woman had been saying. Something about the incredible generosity of his gift, what a wonderful guy he was, how his openhandedness should get the widespread publicity it deserved. Lissa thought she caught something about a Man of the Year award, as well.

Kurt said, sounding short-tempered, "The gift

was from this store and Maximum Sports as a whole. Not from me."

Mindy gave a little trill of laughter. "But that's exactly what I mean, Kurt. Just pretending that it wasn't all your idea is another very big-hearted gesture."

She hasn't got any idea what makes him tick, Lissa thought with a tinge of amusement. Then she pulled herself up short. *And you think you do, Lissa?*

Even if she did understand him far better than Mindy ever could, she warned herself, the talent wasn't likely to get her anywhere. Just because she claimed to have some great insight into his character it didn't mean Kurt would appreciate being analyzed. Probably far from it.

As if he had felt her gaze on him, Kurt ran a hand over the back of his neck and looked over his shoulder toward her. Lissa ducked behind the wind-chime display.

Hannah came up beside her. "What are you doing hiding back here?"

Lissa wondered what Hannah would say if she told the truth. *I'm contemplating how I happened to fall in love with your grandson.* No—that wouldn't be smart at all. Lissa fumbled for an acceptable excuse. "I thought I recognized one of the employees," she said. "He's a basketball player at the university, and he asked me for my phone number once." It was true enough, as far as it went.

She'd noticed almost as soon as they arrived that one of the employees looked very much like one of the athletes who had been hanging around the cloakroom the night of Kurt's banquet.

Kurt's banquet. The night her life had changed— though she'd had no idea of it at the time.

"I don't mind if you get calls," Hannah said absently.

Lissa figured there was no point in explaining about the time and temperature in Winnipeg, or why the athlete just might be nursing a grudge.

"I'm very tired," Hannah went on. "I'm going home now, but there's no need for you to leave the party yet."

"I don't mind at all, Hannah. Just let me grab your coat—did you leave it over in that pile on the billiard tables?"

"Don't forget to say good night to Kurt."

Lissa darted a glance in his direction. "It appears Mindy's taking good care of him," she said dryly. "I'd hate to interrupt when she's on such a roll."

Hannah didn't protest, but followed meekly along to the door. Her unusual mildness drew Lissa's attention away from her own preoccupation.

"Are you really just tired tonight?" she asked suspiciously. "Or are you not feeling well? You still haven't called a doctor, have you?"

"I'll get around to it," Hannah said vaguely.

Lissa ran out into the frost-coated parking lot to

warm up the SUV and bring it to the door, so the winter air wouldn't hurt Hannah's lungs. Then she spent the drive home quietly plotting. Maybe if she waited up tonight to share her concerns with Kurt he would put his foot down....

Are you certain you aren't just looking for an excuse to talk to him? To have any sort of meaningful contact with him at all?

By the time they reached the house Hannah seemed to have regained all her spirit, if not her energy. "I can't have you stuffing your own Christmas stocking, you know," she said. "But if you'll do Kurt's and Janet's for me I'd appreciate it." Hannah sat down by the now-dead fireplace to supervise. "I left the goodies on the table in the library."

Lissa retrieved two huge bags, studied the stockings, and wondered how she was to make everything fit. "Just in case you're putting a shoehorn in my stocking, Hannah, may I have it early? It would make this job a little easier."

"No shoehorn, I'm afraid. I didn't realize you wanted one." Hannah's tongue was obviously just as firmly in her cheek as Lissa's.

By the time Lissa had finished, the two stockings were fat and heavy enough to almost drag down the bright red bricks which anchored them to the mantelshelf. Even Hannah's stocking, though Lissa hadn't added anything to it, had a suspicious bulge in the toe and a very swollen calf—Janet must have been busy while they were gone.

But Lissa's, the only one without a name needle-pointed on it, was still just as limp and empty as when she had hung it last weekend.

She didn't feel sorry for herself, or even left out. She'd been on her own too long for that sort of indulgence. She'd long ago learned to face the painful realities straightforwardly and without excuses.

This was just one more good lesson to remember. When Christmas was over and the holiday break came to an end everything would go back to normal. The generic stocking assigned to Lissa this Christmas would be returned to Hannah's stash of seasonal decorations to be used again some other time, for someone else—or given away, if Hannah found someone who would appreciate all her Christmas treasures. Lissa would return to her classes, her work at the student union, and her boarding house room—or one very much like it—all alone.

The only things she would be able to keep from this precious time would be her memories, and her dreams of what might have been.

Christmas morning was unusually bright and beautiful, and despite the party running late the night before Kurt was up almost as early as the sun. Still yawning, he threw on jeans and a sweater and went downstairs.

His grandmother was already in the living room, tucked up on the couch under a knitted blanket, wearing a fuzzy pink dressing gown and matching slippers. "Are you eager to tear into your presents, Kurt?"

"I'm not six years old anymore, Gran." He poked at the fire and added a log. "Besides, at least I took the time to get dressed. What's your excuse for eagerness? You can't wait to see what Santa brought you?"

"I'm eager to watch Lissa's face. What a good child she's been, waiting patiently for the days to go by."

Kurt wasn't about to admit it, but he was feeling just about the same—impatient to see the glow in Lissa's eyes at what must be her first real Christmas in a long time. He eyed the weighted-down stockings and the pile of brightly wrapped gifts under the tree. "And what a big heart you have, Gran," he said softly.

Janet came in with coffee mugs on a tray. Three of them, Kurt noted. "You're actually going to sit down and join us, Janet?"

The housekeeper sniffed. "No. I brought three because I thought the young lady would be hurrying down so she wouldn't miss out on anything. I have pecan rolls in the oven for breakfast, so I can't dawdle." She set the tray on the table in front of Hannah with a thump, and went back to the kitchen.

"Speaking of missing out on things, you and Lissa left last night before the goodbye gifts were handed out." He went out to the hallway and retrieved two small silvery boxes from the pocket of his overcoat. He tossed one to Hannah and perched the other in the overloaded cuff of Lissa's stocking.

Hannah sat up straight, her excitement palpable as she tested the weight of the box.

"Don't get your hopes up," Kurt said dryly. "It's not a diamond necklace—everybody who was at the store last night got one of these."

Hannah ripped the box open. She was exclaiming over the sterling silver Christmas ornament—the Maximum Sports penguin mascot, wielding a finely crafted tennis racquet and ball, engraved with the store name and date—when Lissa came in.

"You haven't turned on the Christmas carols?" she asked.

She, too, was dressed in jeans and a pullover. With her auburn hair and bright green sweater, Kurt thought she looked a bit like a Christmas package herself—just as intriguing, just as full of secrets, just as much fun to investigate and unwrap....

He especially liked the idea of unwrapping her. He spent a moment enjoying the view as Lissa bent over the stereo set to choose the morning's music. She was still too thin, but how could he ever have thought her to be shapeless?

Finally, Kurt tore his gaze away from her nicely rounded little rear. "We were waiting for you. If you'd been another five minutes I'd have blasted you out with 'Jingle Bells.'"

Or maybe I'd have done something which would have been equally sure to wake you up—even if it didn't involve getting you out of bed.

"The youngest person in the room has to sort out the gifts," Hannah ordered. "It's tradition in the family."

Lissa bit her lip, and Kurt saw a shadow flicker in her eyes. *It's tradition in the family....* But Lissa was obviously remembering she *wasn't* family. He was annoyed with his grandmother for tripping over her tongue like that, saying something which was so carelessly hurtful.

"You sort out the boxes, Lissa," he said. "I'll get the stockings down."

The soft strains of an *a capella* choir mingled with the crackle of the flames as he took down the stockings. He set Janet's on the loveseat, a bit away from the fire, because Janet's stocking was always loaded with chocolate and other goodies which didn't react well to heat. Hannah instantly dumped hers in her lap, and tiny packages spilled out over her blanket. Then Kurt paused to watch Lissa dragging packages out from under the tree. It was a sight well worth considering.

With all the boxes distributed, Lissa dropped cross-legged to the floor in front of the fire, so he set her stocking on the hearthrug in front of her before he took his own back to his chair. He sat down at an angle, where he could see Lissa's face.

Nobody moved.

"Go ahead," Hannah urged. "Dump the stocking and dig in. Unless you want to start with your packages instead?"

"Aren't we waiting for Janet?" Lissa asked.

"She'll be along when she's ready."

Finally Lissa reached out and touched the top bulge in her stocking with a tentative finger, picking up the silvery box Kurt had tucked in just a few minutes before she came downstairs. Her ornament showed the Maximum Sports penguin mascot decked out as a skier with poles braced, crouched for a jump.

"Darn," Kurt said. "I was hoping you'd get the rock climber."

Lissa stroked the sterling silver ski mask with a gentle fingertip. "There's a set?" Her voice was wistful.

"We do four ornaments each year, just for employees."

"I never did ask you why your mascot is a penguin."

Kurt grinned. "His name's Tux. I chose him because he's awkward and unwieldy except in the water."

Lissa frowned. "I don't get it."

"People don't have to be graceful or elegant or professional to enjoy sports, any more than Tux is. On land, he waddles and falls over—but he's a heck of a swimmer. The point is that everybody can find a sport they're good at—even if they're awkward, it's all right."

"Enough with the fairy tales," Hannah interrupted. "Get on with those packages, girl!"

Lissa reluctantly set the silver penguin aside and dug into her stocking. The next item wasn't even wrapped—in fact it was just a simple chocolate orange in a decorative box—but she studied it, sniffed it, and smiled.

Hannah was fidgeting. Kurt didn't know which he was enjoying more—watching Lissa make the most of the holiday, or watching Hannah being driven wild by such care and patience. The longer Lissa took to slit the tape and unfold the paper from each box, the more Hannah bounced on the couch. He found the show quite entertaining to watch.

The stack of discarded paper and empty boxes grew. Kurt unwrapped a package which had no giver's name on the tag—not that it needed one, since it was clear as soon as he saw the title of the book whose idea this gift had been.

"You must have ransacked the bookstores to find this," he said dryly as he held up *The Calculus Cheat Sheet*.

So that was how she'd spent part of the money she'd borrowed from him. Now he was glad he'd indulged his own whimsical side.

He set the book aside and rummaged through Lissa's pile of gifts. "Here, open this one next."

It was small and flat, wrapped in paper emblazoned with Maximum Sports' logo. As she lifted a gold-embossed certificate out of the box, she eyed it warily. "You gave me a ticket for the climbing wall?"

"Not just one ticket. It's a free pass, so you can climb whenever you want."

"Gee, thanks," Lissa said. "It's so thoughtful of you."

He grinned, enjoying her discomfort. "You've been on a ladder so much this week that the climbing wall probably won't even be a challenge. You must be over your fear of heights by now. When would you like to make your first climb?"

"Oh, I think I'll savor the idea for a while first," she said dryly. "Or maybe I'll just wait till you visit again. I'm sure you'll be back sometime in the next decade."

His grandmother was ecstatic over the seed-pearl choker that Kurt had slipped into her stocking. "You've still got the prettiest neck around," he said, kissing her cheek when she thanked him.

But she seemed just as pleased, he noticed, by the pair of Austrian crystal earrings Lissa had given her. She put them on instantly, and leaned forward to point out a package in Lissa's pile. "Open that one next," she said. "I can't wait to see your face."

Lissa's eyes widened and she looked at Kurt, as if begging him to rescue her. With obvious reluctance she picked up the package. Small, flat, and apparently almost weightless, it looked as if it might be a box of stationery. Or…

"What is it, Gran?" he asked lazily. "The deed to the house?"

"No, dear. You should know better than that."

Lissa relaxed visibly and started to pull tape loose from the red foil paper.

"Some things just aren't appropriate Christmas gifts," Hannah went on. "And in any case, I've reconsidered."

Lissa paused. "You have?"

Kurt leaned back and folded his hands behind his head. "Why? You didn't like the idea of a hot tub for eight right out by the neighbors' side door?"

Hannah laughed merrily. "Only if I get to come and use it—and enjoy seeing the shock on their faces. But Lissa's right—if you don't want the house, then I shouldn't saddle you with it."

"So you're staying here?" Kurt asked casually.

"Oh, no, dear. I still want something much smaller, much simpler, with much less responsibility. This solution was Lissa's idea, really. Well, not directly—but when we were choosing charities to donate things to it seemed such a pity that the only thing I could give to the group of unwed mothers she's so attached to was a few skeins of yarn and some knitting needles. Since there haven't been any babies in this family for twenty-five years, I don't have high chairs or cribs to give away."

They must be the only things she doesn't have stuck back in a closet somewhere, just in case she might need them someday.

Lissa shifted, as if the hearthrug had suddenly grown hot under her. "Hannah—"

Lissa had gone pale, Kurt noted. *Because she isn't going to get the house after all?* But he'd swear she'd been sincere all the times she'd said she didn't want it. Besides, Lissa was the most pragmatic female he'd ever run across, and she certainly knew how impractical it would be for a young woman with no job to take on a house the size of Hannah's.

So why was she turning white now, instead of looking relieved?

"Young women in difficult situations need options," Hannah said, "not booties. The more we talked about it, the more I realized Lissa knew what she was talking about when she said if those girls had real choices, they'd make better decisions. Decisions they wouldn't regret later. So, when neither of you seemed to want this big old house, I got to thinking about how it might do as a group home— a place where single mothers could come for a while, rent-free, till they get on their feet. There could be classes in how to be good parents, help to get jobs, a cooperative nursery to take care of the babies while the mothers went out to work so they didn't have to pay for daycare."

"Good idea, Gran," Kurt said. He hardly heard

what he was saying. "Of course there may be a bit of a hitch in how to pay for it all, but—"

Hannah didn't pause. "So as soon as the holiday's over, Lissa, I want you to invite your friend who runs the women's shelter out here, and we'll sit down and talk about it—about how we could make it all work."

Lissa swallowed hard. "Whenever you like, Hannah. But let's talk about it some other time. Aren't you going to open the rest of your gifts?" She reached for another package herself and started to tear off the paper.

Kurt's stomach felt as if he'd just topped the first peak of a rollercoaster and dropped into freefall, without the slightest idea of how he'd gotten on the ride. All his suspicions came rushing back like a tidal wave. *There haven't been any babies in the family for twenty-five years*—as far as his grandmother knew. But was that the truth?

I realized Lissa knew what she was talking about, Hannah had said. *If these girls had real choices, they'd make better decisions. Decisions they wouldn't regret later.*

Lissa knew what she was talking about…*how?* From firsthand experience?

In some situations there aren't any good choices, she had told him once. *You just deal with it and go on, that's all.* It had been the voice of experience speaking then—matter-of-fact, almost toneless, with no pain. Not because there hadn't been any pain involved, but because she was long past feeling it. It had been the voice of a woman who had looked a bad break in the eye, dealt with it, and survived.

That had been the moment when he'd first started to wonder if she was talking about something other than her father's terminal cancer and her own bout of illness. But when he'd confronted her about the possibility of a pregnancy she'd almost ridiculed the idea.

What do you think I did with this supposed infant? I hope you're satisfied that it never happened....
She had assured him there had never been a baby.
Or…had she?

He was struggling to recall exactly what she had and hadn't said when a crash reverberated from the kitchen. It was a full three seconds before Kurt, his reflexes paralyzed by the sudden shocking questions whirling through his mind, realized that the echo of metal clanging, glass shattering, and something heavy thudding to the floor was real.

Janet had taken a fall.

Maybe, he thought, his grandmother had waited just a little too long to make her move into retirement.

Hannah jumped up, untangled herself from her blanket, and rushed toward the kitchen. Lissa was only a couple of steps behind her, but as Hannah vanished around the corner and into the hall Kurt reached out and grabbed Lissa's arm, holding her back.

She skidded to a halt and glared at him. "What are you doing? We should go see what's happened out there!"

"In a minute. I can hear Janet swearing a blue streak—she sounds a whole lot more angry than hurt. Lissa…." He took a deep breath. "About this woman who runs the shelter…"

She couldn't believe her ears. "Can we do this later, Kurt? *After* the crisis is past?"

"No, we can't. How long have you known her?"

"Several years. If you're asking whether she's the sort of person who would take advantage of a kind-hearted old lady who only wants to help girls who are in trouble—"

"No." His eyes were dark, the lines around them deeper than usual, as if he had a sudden, splitting headache. "I just wondered how you'd happened to meet her. And how you know all that stuff you told Gran—about young women and choices, and decisions, and regret."

Lissa bit her lip. The moment Hannah had started talking she'd been afraid of how Kurt might react, what he might say. If he let any of this slip to Hannah it would only cause pain, without doing anyone any good. She had to try to stop it, to convince him. "Are we back to that again? I told you, Kurt—I did not have your baby. I did not give your child up for adoption."

He was silent for a long moment. But not, she thought warily, because he was convinced.

When he finally spoke, his voice was very low. "Those aren't the only possibilities. You never said you weren't pregnant, Lissa. Just that you didn't have a baby."

They say men don't have intuition, she thought. *Well, this one must.* "And that's the truth," she said, as firmly as she could. "I didn't."

"But it's not the whole truth, is it?" He paused, took a deep breath. "Why didn't you tell me you were pregnant?"

In the face of his certainty, Lissa couldn't keep silent any longer. "Because there was nothing to say, Kurt."

All right, you're going to have to tell him. The man's a bulldog; he's not going to back off till he gets an answer.

She took a deep breath and tried to think. *I didn't tell you I was pregnant because I didn't know myself...not for sure.* It was the absolute truth; it would have to do.

"You'd already made up your mind what you were going to do, hadn't you?" His voice held a hard edge. "So what I might have thought about it didn't matter a damn."

"Made up my mind about *what?*" Then it hit

her—the unthinkable thing he was accusing her of—and Lissa reeled from the impact. "If you're saying I had an abortion, Kurt—"

"What else am I supposed to think? *Sometimes there aren't any good choices.* You said that yourself. If there was no baby, no adoption, what else is left? And you didn't even bother to tell me—"

Fury roiled in her stomach. "If I *had* told you I was pregnant, Kurt, what would you have done about it?"

"I sure as hell wouldn't have let you kill my baby." *My baby.*

He had made a bet with his buddies that he could get her to sleep with him, and no doubt he had celebrated with them and collected his winnings. He had given her not a single additional thought. Not then. Not when his buddies had tormented her. Not when she'd vanished from the class.

But if that night of carelessness had resulted in a child…*that* he would have cared about. Not Lissa—she didn't matter. She had never mattered to him. But a baby…

You've always known where you stand with him, Lissa told herself. *Nothing's changed.*

But it *had* changed. Everything had changed. For him to coldly look at her and assume that she was capable of ending a child's life simply because she'd found it inconvenient to be pregnant….

Rage rose in her. She was damned if she'd beg him to believe her. He had appointed himself judge and jury and issued a verdict. The overwhelming urge to hurt him just as deeply as he'd hurt her swept over her.

Her conscience whispered, *A lie is still a lie. No matter how much he deserves to be wounded, you shouldn't sink to lying to him.*

But the words were out before she could think it through. "Sure—that's what happened," she said coolly. "You're always right, aren't you, Kurt? But then it wasn't a baby. Not really. It was a nuisance, that's all."

The instant the words were out she hated herself for saying them—though not because they had hurt him. She still felt he deserved all the pain she could inflict because he'd assumed she could do such a heinous thing.

What she regretted was that in her fury she'd soiled the memory of her child—the baby she was morally certain she had carried for just a few brief weeks. So short a time, in fact, that a pregnancy test hadn't yet shown up positive when the bleeding had started and wouldn't stop....

"Kurt," she said desperately. "I'm sorry. Let me explain—"

His face was like stone. "Sorry you did it? Or sorry I found out?"

Hopelessness swept over her, but she was taking a breath to try again when Hannah came back into the room.

"It's a pity," she said cheerfully, "but there won't be pecan rolls for breakfast. Janet's wrist gave out as she was transferring them to a plate and she dropped the whole lot on the floor. Kurt, you'll have to run down to the grocery and get some donuts." She looked from one of them to the other and frowned. "Are you two all right?"

"Sure," Lissa said. "Fine. I'll go help clean up."

"That's a great idea." Kurt's voice was hard. "You're so experienced at getting rid of messes, Lissa. Aren't you?"

CHAPTER TEN

KURT SEIZED HIS coat from the closet and stormed out of the house. The silence he left behind was thick, the atmosphere so heavy that it was like trying to breathe underwater.

"Do you want to talk about it?" Hannah asked.

As if, Lissa thought, this was a simple lovers' spat. *Kiss and make up….*

"No." She shuddered uncontrollably; chills were coursing up and down her spine. She wanted to follow Kurt, explain, but how could she? "No, I don't want to talk about it. If you'd like me to go away, Hannah—"

"Where would you go?" Hannah asked practically. "It's Christmas Day."

The reminder would have brought tears to Lissa's eyes if she hadn't been in too much pain to cry. How could she and Kurt have forgotten the holiday, and how much it meant to Hannah? "I'm sorry to ruin your Christmas."

"It wouldn't be the first time." Hannah's voice was matter-of-fact. "When Kurt's parents were still together—" She seemed to think better of saying it. "If you'd give Janet a hand in the kitchen, I'd appreciate it."

Lissa nodded, and looked over her shoulder as she left the living room. Hannah was already standing by the sideboard, sherry bottle in hand. Lissa might have joined her—only for her the sherry wouldn't have been nearly strong enough.

Still-steaming pecan rolls lay scattered on the kitchen floor in a puddle of caramel sauce, absurdly crowned with shards of the milk-glass cakestand that Janet had been transferring them to.

By the time the mess was gathered up and the floor scrubbed, Lissa was starting to wonder if Kurt was going to come back at all. But just as she was wringing the last of the sticky sauce from the mop the side door banged open and he came into the kitchen, two big white bakery bags clutched in one hand.

I'm sorry I let my temper get the best of me, she wanted to say. *I shouldn't have lied to you. I should have told you that I think I had a miscarriage so early that there's nothing to prove I was ever pregnant at all.* But it was too late for that; he'd never believe her now.

He came straight toward her, and the iciness in his eyes chilled her blood. "We aren't going to ruin Gran's Christmas." There was a thread of steel in his voice.

"Now's a fine time for you to consider that." Deliberately she let a hint of sarcasm creep into her tone. It was better than breaking down in tears. "But I suppose an afterthought is better than nothing. What's your plan?"

"I pretend you don't exist, you pretend I don't exist, and we get through the day the best we can."

She felt compelled to say, "I've already offered to leave."

"Don't bother. I've bought a ticket. I'll be flying out late this afternoon."

He was so anxious to get away that he didn't even want to wait for his private jet to pick him up. It was no surprise that he wanted to avoid her. Still, for her own sake there was something she had to say.

"Just for the record," she said, trying to hold back the emotion. "I didn't have an abortion." She shoved the mop into the tall cupboard beside the sink and left the room without a backward look.

Just get through the day, Lissa told herself. *Just get through this day and you'll never have to see him again.*

The winter felt endless, and spring was late, wet, and cold. Some days it seemed to Lissa that the sun would never shine again. But the months went by, and she plodded through the last of her classes and the last of her shifts at the student union, and eventually she reached a level of acceptance and almost peace. Whatever Kurt thought of her, it no longer mattered.

Her graduation day, late in May, was perfect—sunny, but not too warm. The scent of lilacs drifted across the campus from the rows of groomed bushes near the quadrangle where the ceremony was being held, and the long tassel on her mortarboard stirred in the breeze and tickled her ear as she half listened to the speaker.

Perhaps, she thought, it had been silly to dress up in cap and gown and go through the motions of the formal ceremony. She'd be a graduate just the same, whether she walked across the stage or not, and she could have spent the day polishing up her job applications. Between working, studying, and writing her senior project, the not-so-small problem of what she was going to do next had not gotten the attention it deserved.

And it wasn't as if there was a proud family waiting in the stands to cheer her accomplishment.

She hadn't invited Hannah to the ceremony. In fact, Lissa hadn't seen her for several weeks—and even then they'd been meeting with the director of the women's shelter, so the only subject had been the transformation of Hannah's house to make it accommodate more than half a dozen young women and their babies. But, even if the agenda had been less crucial, Lissa was reasonably certain Hannah wouldn't have mentioned Kurt. In fact, since he'd left the house late on Christmas afternoon, Hannah had not once brought up his name—even during the following week, when his presence had still been palpable and the scent of his aftershave still hiding in unexpected corners of his grandmother's house, lurking as if to ambush Lissa.

Lissa didn't know what Kurt had told his grand-mother—if anything—about that last fight. She was fairly sure he hadn't breathed a word, and that Hannah was still as much in the dark as she'd been on Christmas Day, when they'd been frigidly polite to each other over the dinner table. For if he'd told his grandmother about Lissa and his suspicions that she'd deliberately ended a pregnancy then he'd have had to admit that he was the man who'd caused it.

Not long after the pumpkin pie was cut Kurt had left for the airport, and Lissa hadn't heard from him since. Not that she'd expected to, though for a while she'd felt the clench of fear in her gut whenever she went to work and found a message waiting for her at the union—because, she thought, that was the only place he'd have known to reach her.

But as the weeks had gone by she'd gradually come to accept that it was really over. She was still angry at him for judging her, hurt that he could have thought her capable of such a thing. And she still regretted that she'd lied to him—even though she knew he wouldn't have believed her if she'd told the truth right then.

She wished the end could have been less painful

and less public, and that Hannah hadn't walked into the crossfire and been hurt. She wished that she could still consider the old woman a friend, not just an acquaintance.

And, in a few dark, middle-of-the-night contemplations, she'd found herself wishing all over again that things had turned out differently. Not because having his baby would have kept Kurt in her life—she wouldn't have wanted him there if he'd had to be forced, and he'd made it clear enough that nothing short of a child would have drawn him to her. But, as complicated as her life would have been under those circumstances, she would have had her reward in watching her child grow.

Instead, she'd barely begun to suspect the existence of a pregnancy, much less come to terms with how she would manage life with a baby, before it had all been over.

But the time was past for all those sorts of thoughts. This was the end of a long and difficult chunk of her life, and it was time for a fresh start.

The university president called her name. Lissa held her head high as she climbed the steps to the temporary stage set up in the center of the quadrangle and walked across to receive her diploma. There were a few cheers; she saw her fellow workers at the student union in a clump right down front, yelling, and her heart warmed. The dean of the business college presented her diploma, shook her hand, and whispered, "Congratulations, Lissa. You have a bright future, I know."

The parade of names was the very end of the ceremony, and as the black-gowned graduates came down the steps at the far end of the stage, diploma in hand, they moved off to the side, out onto the quadrangle where they could mingle and celebrate.

The stairs were makeshift, and she had to watch that the heel of her shoe didn't slide down into the metal grid, or that her toe didn't catch in the hem of the long black gown. Going down was harder than ascending had been, and she was grateful for the arm which was offered in support as she climbed off the stage.

Until she drew her next breath and caught the scent of an aftershave she'd thought she would never smell again.

Her hand stilled on Kurt's arm.

"Congratulations," he said.

She nodded. It was the only thanks she could manage; for her life, she couldn't have forced a word out.

Though she was off the stairs, once more on solid ground, the grass seemed to sway under her, and Lissa was afraid to trust her feet. As if he'd read her mind, Kurt pulled his arm closer to his body, trapping her hand, and drew her away from the stage.

She looked around. "Is Hannah here?" Her voice was little more than a breath.

Kurt shook his head. "Since you didn't officially invite her, she couldn't get a seat—and she didn't think she could stand through the whole ceremony."

"It was nice of you to come as her delegate." *Let's make it clear right up front—you're not here because of me, and I know it.*

"Would you like punch and cookies?" Kurt asked.

"No—I'm not staying for the reception."

"Because you have too much to do?" His tone was light, conversational.

As if he cares. "Yes, I thought I'd take the rest of the day off to do some serious relaxing before I get down to the task of finding a job."

"Then my timing was perfect." Suddenly he sounded serious. "Lissa, I want...I *need* to talk to you."

"Oh, I think you said everything that was on your mind at Christmas, Kurt. Pardon me if I'd rather not sit through a repetition. So, thanks again for coming. Tell Hannah I'll talk to her sometime, and..." She pulled the mortarboard off her head and ran her fingers through her hair. *And don't send me a Christmas card; if I want to know what's going on with you I'll just read the business magazines.*

"Lissa." His voice was quiet. "I'm going to say what I came here to tell you. You can stand here and listen to me, or you can walk away and I'll follow you and shout as loud as I have to, to make sure you hear. So it's up to you, really. Do you want to keep this between us, or not?"

That would make a nice scene for the crowd—on the stage, the university president still reading off the last half of the graduates' names, while mere feet away Kurt boomed out—what? More accusations?

A crowd had gathered around the refreshment table, and newcomers from the stage sidestepped Kurt and Lissa to head in that direction. Off to one side of the quadrangle lay an almost deserted path, and Lissa moved toward it. "Why right now?" she said wearily. "It's been months, Kurt. Why did you have to ruin my graduation day?"

"I didn't intend to ruin it. I came to tell you I'm sorry."

She turned to face him. "Sorry for what? There are so many possibilities I don't have any idea where you might begin."

He winced. "Let's start with the biggest one, then. I'm sorry that I accused you of having an abortion."

She thought about it for a moment, not quite sure what he was saying. Was he sorry he'd believed it, or only sorry that he'd voiced the thought?

"I suppose I'd have to call it temporary insanity," he said. "What happened to me on Christmas, I mean. Everything seemed to fit—what you'd said to Gran, the whole idea about the home, the fact that you'd been very careful what you'd said to me. You never exactly told me that you *hadn't* been pregnant, you know."

"I couldn't assure you of something I didn't know myself, Kurt."

But he didn't seem to have heard her. "You only said that you hadn't given up a baby for adoption. Suddenly all of that seemed to fall into place in my head, and the pieces formed a picture—one I didn't like. One I didn't want to believe. But when I confronted you, you didn't deny it. And the look on your face—"

To his already suspicious eyes, she realized, she must have looked and sounded guilty. No surprise there, because she'd *felt* guilty—even though she had done nothing wrong—simply because she'd kept her own suspicions to herself for six long years.

"Not that it excuses what I said to you. Lissa, I'm sorry the idea ever crossed my mind. It didn't occur to me then that there was yet another possibility—that you'd miscarried. That's what happened, isn't it?"

She hesitated. "I think so."

Kurt frowned. "What do you mean, you *think?*"

"It all happened so quickly. As soon as I began to suspect I might be pregnant, I got a test kit. The results said I wasn't, but the instructions made it clear that if it was too early the test wouldn't show up as positive. So I was going to take it again in a few days, but before I could I started bleeding, and…well, it was all over. So I've never really known…even though in my heart I was pretty sure."

"You looked so guilty. And—I wasn't thinking clearly, that's all."

"I'd noticed that," she said dryly.

"But when I finally stopped letting myself be blinded by anger and thought it through, I knew that had to be the answer. If you had been pregnant, you might not have told me—"

"As if you'd have been eager to hear that sort of news."

"But you wouldn't have acted in your own selfish interests. Not if it would hurt someone else."

She supposed she should be pleased that he'd finally worked it out. "I'm glad you at least got that much straight. How long did it take you, did you say?"

"A while. A month or so. I was pretty angry." He paused. "So were you, or you wouldn't have told me that raft of lies."

"Don't try to shift the blame, Kurt."

"I'm not. I take full responsibility for that, too. If I hadn't been such a—"

She could think of several words which fit the situation, but Kurt seemed to conclude that none of them was quite severe enough as a description.

"I attacked you," he said quietly. "I hurt you in the worst possible way. It just took me a while to realize why you would admit to something like that when it wasn't true. But of course you fought back—you wanted to hurt me."

"I'm not proud of what I said," she admitted. "I didn't help things, did I? But even if it took you a full month to figure all this out, why wait till now to talk to me?"

He looked down at the toe of his wingtip and drew an invisible line on the sidewalk. "I know it sounds like I was too scared to face you. And perhaps I was, for a while—because I knew what a horrible thing I'd done to you, and I couldn't imagine you being willing to talk to me no matter what I did. Last time, you wouldn't listen at all."

"By *last time,* you mean when you caught up with me that day after calculus class? The day after we… You didn't try very hard to talk to me then, Kurt."

"Maybe we've both learned something in the last six years."

Maybe, she thought doubtfully. Though if he'd called her up anytime this spring she might have slammed the phone down. She'd been plenty angry, too. Even this afternoon she hadn't wanted to hear him out.

"But I couldn't just let it ride," Kurt went on. "Whether you listened to me or not, I had to at least tell you I was sorry—for everything. At the same time, I knew everything you'd been through the last few years in trying to finish school, and I didn't want to risk that. As long as you were doing all right, I didn't want to upset you all over again. So I waited till the semester was done—till today. And I thought if I approached you in public…"

Shanghaiing her was more like it. "I see."

"If I've done the wrong thing by coming to talk to you, I'm sorry—but at least by waiting I didn't throw you off course again and keep you from graduating."

"Very thoughtful of you. You said you knew I was doing all right? How? Oh, from Hannah, I suppose."

"No. Gran wouldn't so much as breathe your name. I called up the dean of the business school."

The dean—the man who had just shaken her hand up on stage and murmured, *You have a bright future*. Much he knew about it, Lissa thought. "I suppose he read you my report card in return for a nice contribution?"

"Not exactly. But he did agree to keep an eye on you—and he seemed to be impressed by what he saw."

Lissa said dryly, "He was probably only impressed because you were the one who was asking about me. He loves to use Maximum Sports as a good example—of everything."

"What are you going to do next, Lissa?"

He was finished, she realized. The apology was over, the discussion complete, and now he was moving on to civil chit-chat for a few moments before saying goodbye. "Look for a job. So far I haven't had anything but nibbles."

"If you're interested, there's a position with Maximum Sports."

"That wasn't a hint for you to hire me, Kurt. Besides, I'm terrible at sales, and I'd scare people away from the climbing wall—so, thanks, but no."

"It's corporate," he said. "I'd like you to set up that new simplified tracking system you told me you could create."

It would be her dream job, and for a moment Lissa let herself wallow in the thought of how perfect it all could be.

"I feel bad about the internship," Kurt went on. "You kept your part of the bargain—Gran's finally moved out of the house, and everything's settled—but I didn't keep mine. I wanted to, but I thought if I offered you a job—or suggested I pay your rent—you'd throw it in my face after what I'd said to you."

"I might have," she admitted. "And I didn't exactly accomplish what you wanted, anyway. It took Hannah all spring to get the house mostly cleared out, and even though they're remodeling now, she's still got the china stacked in an upstairs closet because she swears you're going to want it someday—so I didn't figure you owed me anything."

"Well, that's past. Now that we've got things straightened out...."

Oh, yes. Everything's just peachy, now.

"What about the job, Lissa? A real job, I mean—not an internship."

She eyed him narrowly. "I thought you said the dean didn't read you my report card."

His eyebrows furrowed. "What are you talking about?"

"Never mind. It's nothing. Thanks for the offer—but I don't think so, Kurt."

It was the only thing she could say. Working near him, working for him, but not being with him, would be more than she could bear.

He nodded, obviously not surprised that she'd turned him down. She wondered if there was a flicker of relief deep inside him. If so, at least he'd had the decency and self-control not to show it.

They'd reached the far edge of the quadrangle, where the shade of a row of pine trees kept the sidewalk even cooler than the grassy expanse they'd crossed. The campus boundary was just ahead, and beyond that was only a neighborhood of student housing. There was no further excuse to linger, so she tipped her head back and looked directly up at him. "Anything else you want to get off your chest before I go, Kurt?"

He took his time answering. "I've really ruined things, haven't I?"

She wanted to say, *Yes. You ruined everything.* But she had ached so long and so deeply that she was too guarded to admit that there had been anything between them at all, anything which could be ruined. So she only shrugged and turned away, hoping that she could get out of sight before she broke down and cried.

"At least let me walk you home, Lissa."

She clenched her fists on the hard leather binder that held her diploma until her knuckles ached. But there really was no reason she could give for not allowing him to share a public sidewalk with her on a beautiful spring day, so she shrugged and started off, setting a brisk pace.

"You haven't asked why it was so easy for me to convince myself that there had been a baby," he mused.

"Oh? Your being a bit paranoid wasn't enough of a reason?"

"I don't think so. And neither was remembering that you'd supposedly been sick that spring. You see…what I finally realized was that part of me *wanted* there to have been a baby."

The admission was so startling that she tripped over thin air. Kurt grabbed her arm to steady her and didn't let go. "My parents…." he said slowly. "They didn't fight all the time because they both wanted me, they fought because they didn't."

There was no pain in his voice, only acknowledgment of the truth. But she felt his hurt nevertheless. "I'm sorry, Kurt."

He shrugged. "They only got married because I was on the way. I've always thought it would have been better if they hadn't bothered."

She listened to the rhythm of their footsteps, almost in tune against the concrete. "I don't understand. If it was so bad for you, why would you want another child to feel like a burden?"

"Because it would have been different. I'm not my parents."

She nodded. "But…"

"I would have wanted my baby. And when for that instant of time I thought that there had been a child and I'd lost him—or her —"

It wasn't a baby, she'd said to him. *It was a nuisance.* It had been a blow struck in anger, a lie told in a moment when she'd have done anything in her power to wound him. Now she wondered how many times he'd heard *himself* called a nuisance by the people who should have loved him most.

No wonder he'd turned to stone when she'd said it. She couldn't have found a way to hurt him more.

He looked down at her, almost as if he were seeing her for the first time. "I went crazy—I'm not making an excuse, because there isn't any. If I'd only stopped to consider I'd have known you couldn't do that—but I didn't take the time to think it through. Lissa, I'd give my right arm if I could go back and relive that fifteen minutes."

Something deep inside her relaxed—something which had been so tense since Christmas that she had grown used to it, even begun to think it was normal. "Oh, not the right arm, Kurt," she murmured. "It would make climbing that wall much too difficult."

He frowned at her as if he didn't appreciate the feeble effort at humor. "It's taken me six years to figure out what's wrong with me. Six long years to figure out that what happened between us that night was no accident."

She wanted to snort. "Of course it wasn't an accident. You planned it."

He shook his head.

"Come on. You can't deny there was a bet."

"It wasn't what you thought. I didn't set out to go to bed with you. I told one of the guys that you were going to tutor me, and he started making jokes about how I must want something more than a calculus lesson, and I said, yeah, sure, I had all kinds of plans. It was the sort of thing all stupid young guys say when they're trying to sound macho in front of their buddies. Before I saw what was happening everybody knew about it. I tried to squelch the talk, but then after that incredible night…."

He had thought it was incredible, too?

Calling it incredible doesn't necessarily mean he thought it was wonderful, Lissa reminded herself.

"At first I was too stunned to think. Nothing like that had ever happened to me before. But you were like a startled rabbit —jumpy and anxious, in such a hurry to get out of my room that of course I said all the wrong things. Did all the wrong things." He sighed. "And by the next day, we both must have been giving off vibes—because it was obvious to everyone what had happened. Then there was no stopping the gossip."

And as soon as she'd heard about the bet she'd refused to speak to him at all....

Kurt had been a fool, there was no argument about that. But so had she. They had let their passion carry them away, long before their tentative friendship had been strong enough to stand the pressure. Then, in their proud refusal to be the first one to confess—in their fear of being embarrassed if feelings turned out not to be mutual—they'd squashed any possibility of finding out if their attraction could turn into something more lasting.

At least now there's no more need to wonder what happened. We did it to ourselves, in equal measures.

"Then you wouldn't even give me the time of day," Kurt went on. "So I assumed that it hadn't been so wonderful for you after all, and I stopped trying. But even while I was telling myself that women couldn't be trusted, that you'd slept with me and then turned your back—"

"Wait a minute. *I* turned my back?"

"I didn't say I was right, Lissa, just that it's what I thought back then. It hurt me, that you had walked away without seeming to care. And I was still hurting when I saw you again at the cloakroom that night, when you told me to get lost. By then, I'd buried it so deeply that I didn't recognize what was happening—but that's why I was so nasty and suspicious at first. And when I began to suspect that you'd been pregnant—and hadn't even told me…."

She sighed. "I would have told you, Kurt—if I'd been sure. But there was never anything definite to tell you. I certainly wasn't going to walk up to you and say, *I just wanted you to know I thought I might be pregnant but I'm not.*"

He smiled a little. "Yeah, I can see that. Lissa, I know it must have been a relief to you when it was all over…but I almost wish it had been different."

She stopped at the foot of the steps outside her boarding house. "It wasn't a relief," she said, almost under her breath. "Well, this is the end of the road."

He didn't look at her but at the façade of the house, and for an instant she saw it through his eyes. The porch was even more rickety than it had been at Christmas. The stairs sagged. The paint was peeling off the front door, and a panel of glass that had been loose then was gone now, replaced by a board.

Kurt's jaw tightened. "I wanted so much to take you out of here. But I messed that up, too."

She was so glad that he hadn't picked up on her admission—or at least she told herself she was glad—that she was almost giddy. "Oh, really? Then why did you raise such a fuss when Hannah tried to give me her house?"

"Because I didn't want you to have it," he admitted.

"Seems a little contradictory, Kurt."

"I didn't want the house to get in the way. I didn't want it to be a possession to come between us, something to fight over the way my parents fought over everything." He turned her to face him, his hands tight on the shoulders of her black gown. "I didn't want you to get attached to the house—because I wanted to take you with me."

Her heart was suddenly beating in a staccato rhythm she'd never felt before. "And I suppose that's why you offered to rent an apartment for me here, right? You aren't making sense, Kurt."

"I know I'm not. Give me a chance, Lissa. This is hard for me."

She looked up at him for a long moment. There was something about his expression, a turbulence in his eyes… "I'm going inside."

His grip tightened almost painfully for an instant, and then he let her go. "All right. Thanks for listening. I—Can I call you sometime?"

"I just meant you can come in—if you want." She climbed the steps, trying not to care whether he would follow—and knowing by the way her body reacted that he was right behind her.

She unlocked the new deadbolt on her door. "I've got a microwave now, so I can heat water for coffee or tea." She laid her diploma and mortarboard aside and unzipped the black gown, laying it carefully over the back of the futon sofa.

He shrugged. "Coffee, I guess. If you don't mind the bother."

At least it was something to do with her hands. She poured water from a carafe into two mugs and set them into the tiny microwave, watching from the corner of her eye as he walked across the room to the mantel.

Her little Christmas tree was long packed away, but in the center of the mantel sat Tux—the penguin mascot in skiing gear that he'd given her at Christmas.

She knew the instant Kurt saw the silver ornament, for he released a long, startled breath. "You kept him." He turned to face her and his eyes held a new light. "You didn't throw him away. Why, Lissa?"

"Because he's silver."

"Only plated. Not enough to be valuable. You should have jumped up and down on him, to get even with me."

She took the mugs out and stirred instant coffee powder into the hot water. "It wasn't Tux's fault."

"No," he said softly. "It was mine. Every bit of it. You said a minute ago that it wasn't a relief to find out you weren't pregnant. Why, Lissa? Because you wanted a baby?"

Your baby. But something prevented her from saying it. If she admitted how much she cared about him and he didn't return the feeling.... It *seemed* that he was telling her he cared, and yet....

Have you learned nothing at all? she asked

herself. Wasn't this exactly what they'd done six years ago? Then they'd both been afraid to be the first to speak, and so neither of them had said anything. Now—it might not make a difference, but at least she would know that she had done her best, that she had told the truth even if it caused her pain.

"I should have been relieved," she said. "It would have been…very difficult. And yet…. I've tried to convince myself over the years that I couldn't have been pregnant at all, that it was only my imagination, that there was nothing to mourn. But…I couldn't forget."

"The baby?"

She bit her lip. "No, Kurt. I couldn't forget you."

He didn't move. Had she torn herself in two for nothing?

His voice was very soft. "You asked me once why, if so many women were after me, one of them hadn't tripped me up yet. You're the reason, Lissa. None of those women was you."

Her nerves were jangling. "If you're expecting me to believe that you've nursed some sort of crush on me for the last six years—"

"It's true. That night in the cloakroom, even before I knew who you were, I was ready to punch out the jocks who were hanging around drooling over you. You were already mine, and somewhere deep in my gut I knew it."

"Then I told you to get lost."

"And even that didn't stop me from wanting you. It wasn't until you said you didn't want to date me—"

She wiped up a few drops of coffee and dropped the paper napkin into the wastebasket. "What I was really saying was that I didn't want to pretend."

His eyes narrowed. Very slowly, he set his mug down, and then reached for hers and put it safely out of the way. "What about if it's for real, Lissa? All of it?"

For real. Was he truly telling her what she had so longed to hear?

"Being raised by parents like mine doesn't spawn much confidence in catchphrases like *happily ever after* and *till death do us part,*" he mused.

"I understand, Kurt—"

"But when I look at you, Lissa, I believe in those things. I love you."

She wanted to cry, to laugh, to yell at him for keeping her in suspense so long.

"I know I haven't done a very good job of showing it. I'll make up for it, I swear—"

"Yes," she said. "You certainly will. Starting now."

He pulled her against him, and his mouth came down on hers with a hunger which told her more than words could say.

Eventually he let her go, still cupping his hands around her face, and just looked at her for a while. Then he draped an arm around her shoulders and said, "We've got a lot to talk about. But let's not do it here. Would you like some real coffee? This stuff is cold."

"That's not my fault," she pointed out. "Where are we going? Hannah's place?"

"You're kidding, right? Have you seen her new apartment? There's no place for a guest, so I checked into a hotel."

"That's convenient," she murmured.

"Very. They have excellent room service…. Then in a few days…" He sounded anxious. "You'll come with me, Lissa? You'll work with me? And you'll marry me and take over all Gran's china?"

A last doubt flared deep inside her. "I don't know, Kurt. I love you, honestly I do—but I'm scared."

His eyes were full of pain. "Because I wouldn't listen to you. Because I wouldn't believe you, or trust that you couldn't do something so dreadful. It won't happen again, I swear it. I know saying it doesn't prove anything—so take as much time as you need to be sure. Just give me the right to convince you, Lissa. That's all I'm asking for right now."

Slowly, she nodded. He lifted her hand and kissed each fingertip as gently as the touch of a butterfly's wing, and she relaxed, feeling safe in his arms. "Then—all right."

"You mean all right you'll marry me? Or all right I can start convincing you?" He didn't wait for an answer. But a bit later he broke off the kiss and held her just a little distance from him. "And you'll set up that tracking system for me?" He was suddenly all business.

Lissa had to laugh—for the abrupt shift from lover to businessman was somehow more convincing than any number of sweet words could have been. "You're impossible, Kurt."

"I'll make you vice-president of marketing."

"What is this? Nepotism?" It felt so good to be able to tease him.

"Of course not. I really do need that tracking system, you know—the sooner the better."

"Is this afternoon quick enough?"

He frowned. "It can't be that simple."

"Of course it's not. I've spent all semester writing it—it was my senior project."

He rubbed his temple as if it hurt. "After all the pain I've caused you, you spent the whole semester trying to improve my business?"

"Sort of." She didn't look straight at him. "Though I never intended to give it to you. And I have to admit I started out to prove your business plan was badly thought out and you were going about it all wrong—"

He laughed and pulled her closer. "So that's what you meant about your report card. You thought the dean told me about your senior project."

"He was my adviser. I told you that he thinks Maximum Sports is the greatest. Besides, I know firsthand that you can be very persuasive when you're determined to get what you want."

"Well, yes," he admitted. "But take all the time you need—tomorrow will be fine."

Then he was kissing her again, and she quickly forgot about inventory tracking. "Kurt, about that incredible night we spent together…." Her voice was very small. "What if it isn't so incredible now?"

He tucked her head under his chin and let his hand drift over her hair. Then he smiled down at her with mischief dancing in his eyes and said, "It will be. But I've got a surefire idea—let's make it a bet. Then we can't possibly go wrong."

MILLS & BOON®

Live the emotion

Tender romance™

HAVING THE FRENCHMAN'S BABY *by Rebecca Winters*

The Brides of Bella Lucia

Rachel Valentine is wine-buyer for the exclusive *Bella Lucia* restaurants and her relationship with wine-maker Luc Chartier should be strictly business… Their one night of passion is followed by a shocking revelation about Luc's past. Then Rachel discovers she's pregnant…

FOUND: HIS FAMILY *by Nicola Marsh*

A businesswoman and single mum, Aimee is happy. But now her little boy, Toby, is sick, and Aimee needs the one person she thought she would never see again, his father, Jed. When Jed left five years ago he hadn't known Aimee was pregnant. Now Jed is determined to make up for lost time…

SAYING YES TO THE BOSS *by Jackie Braun*

Regina Bellini doesn't believe in love at first sight. Then she is forced to work for the man who makes her heart stand still, Dane Conlan, and the attraction between them is undeniable. Perhaps even enough to tempt her into saying yes to her boss, in spite of what – and who – stands between them.

COMING HOME TO THE COWBOY *by Patricia Thayer*

The Brides of Bella Lucia

Torn between two families, New Yorker Rebecca Valentine has lived her life for her work. But now it's time to put her career second and herself first. With one final assignment to complete, Rebecca goes to millionaire cowboy Mitchell Tucker's ranch. Rebecca realises Mitchell has what she really wants – a family…

On sale 4th August 2006

Available at WHSmith, Tesco, ASDA, Borders, Eason, Sainsbury's and most bookshops

www.millsandboon.co.uk

Join Mills & Boon® Tender Romance™ as the doors to the Bella Lucia restaurant empire are opened!

We bring you...

The Brides of Bella Lucia

A family torn apart by secrets, reunited by marriage

**There's double the excitement in August 2006!
Meet twins Rebecca and Rachel Valentine**

Having the Frenchman's Baby – Rebecca Winters
Coming Home to the Cowboy – Patricia Thayer

**Then join Emma Valentine as she gets a
royal welcome in September**
The Rebel Prince – Raye Morgan

Take a trip to the Outback and meet Jodie this October
Wanted: Outback Wife – Ally Blake

**On cold November nights catch up with
newcomer Daniel Valentine**
Married under the Mistletoe – Linda Goodnight

Snuggle up with sexy Jack Valentine over Christmas
Crazy About the Boss – Teresa Southwick

**In the New Year join Melissa as she heads off
to a desert kingdom**
The Nanny and the Sheikh – Barbara McMahon

**And don't miss the thrilling end to the Valentine
saga in February 2007**
The Valentine Bride – Liz Fielding

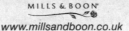

MILLS & BOON®

www.millsandboon.co.uk

The child she
loves…is
his child.

And now he
knows…

THE SEVEN YEAR SECRET BY ROZ DENNY FOX

Mallory Forester's daughter needs a transplant. But there's
only one person left to turn to – Liddy's father. Mallory hasn't
seen Connor in seven years, and now she has to tell him he's a
father…with a chance to save his daughter's life!

HIS DADDY'S EYES BY DEBRA SALONEN

Judge Lawrence Bishop spent a weekend in the arms of a sexy
stranger two years ago and he's been looking for her ever since.
He discovers she's dead, but *her baby son* is living with his aunt,
Sara Carsten. Ren does the maths and realises he's got to see
pretty Sara, talk to her and go from there…

Look for more *Little Secrets* coming in August!

On sale 7th July 2006

The child she loves…is his child.

And now he knows…

HER SISTER'S CHILDREN BY ROXANNE RUSTAND

When Claire Worth inherits her adorable but sad five-year-old twin nieces, their fourteen-year-old brother and a resort on Lake Superior, her life is turned upside down. Then Logan Matthews, her sister's sexy first husband turns up – will he want to break up Claire's fledgling family, when he discovers that Jason is his son?

WILD CAT AND THE MARINE BY JADE TAYLOR

One night of passion doesn't make a marriage, but it could make a child. A beautiful daughter. Cat Darnell hadn't been able to trample on her lover's dream and kept her secret. Joey was the light of her life. And now, finally, Jackson Gray was coming home…was going to meet his little girl…

On sale 4th August 2006

"I was fifteen when my mother finally told me the truth about my father. She didn't mean to. She meant to keep it a secret forever. If she'd succeeded it might have saved us all."

When a hauntingly familiar stranger knocks on Roberta Dutreau's door, she is compelled to begin a journey of self-discovery leading back to her childhood. But is she ready to know the truth about what happened to her, her best friend Cynthia and their mothers that tragic night ten years ago?

16th June 2006

MIRA

"People look at me and they see this happy face, but inside I'm screaming. It's just that no-one hears me."

While breaking the news of Princess Diana's death to millions, reporter Isabel Murphy unravels on live television. *But Inside I'm Screaming* is the heart-rending tale of her struggle to regain the life that everyone thought she had.

21st July 2006

4 FREE

BOOKS AND A SURPRISE GIFT!

We would like to take this opportunity to thank you for reading this Mills & Boon® book by offering you the chance to take FOUR more specially selected titles from the Tender Romance™ series absolutely FREE! We're also making this offer to introduce you to the benefits of the Reader Service™—

- ★ **FREE home delivery**
- ★ **FREE gifts and competitions**
- ★ **FREE monthly Newsletter**
- ★ **Exclusive Reader Service offers**
- ★ **Books available before they're in the shops**

Accepting these FREE books and gift places you under no obligation to buy. you may cancel at any time. even after receiving your free shipment. Simply complete your details below and return the entire page to the address below. You don't even need a stamp!

YES! Please send me 4 free Tender Romance books and a surprise gift. I understand that unless you hear from me. I will receive 6 superb new titles every month for just £2.80 each. postage and packing free. I am under no obligation to purchase any books and may cancel my subscription at any time. The free books and gift will be mine to keep in any case.

N6ZED

Ms/Mrs/Miss/Mr .... Initials ....

BLOCK CAPITALS PLEASE

Surname ....

Address ....

....

.... Postcode ....

Send this whole page to:
UK: FREEPOST CN81, Croydon, CR9 3WZ